WE NEED TO TALK

JONATHAN CRANE

Published in 2021
by Lightning Books Ltd
Imprint of Eye Books Ltd
29A Barrow Street
Much Wenlock
Shropshire
TF13 6EN

www.lightning-books.com

ISBN: 9781785632389
Copyright © Jonathan Crane 2021

Cover by Ifan Bates
Typeset in Bembo and Brandon Grotesque

'Josh' was originally published as 'What's wrong with carpets?' in *Short Fiction in Theory and Practice*, Volume 9, No 2, October 2019.

British Library Cataloguing in Publication Data
A catalogue record for this book is available from the British Library.

Printed by CPI Group (UK) Ltd, Croydon CR0 4YY

MARTIN & BRIDGET

Everyone was talking at once.

'…thin end of the wedge…'

'…single mothers pushing prams…'

'…degrading a respectable neighbourhood…'

Martin looked around the table. They were all there: the hosts, Clive and Susan Saunders; Dr Hugh McFarlane and his wife, Jacqui; Phil Bishop, civil servant, and the artistic Lydia Dixon. They called themselves Fight for Sudleigh; they were discussing the proposed development at the top of the road.

'…destroy the rural character…'

'…push down house prices…'

'…what about the dormice?'

Martin pulled at the dark hairs on the back of his hand.

'And what's Bridget going to do about it?' Phil asked,

forcefully prodding the table.

Martin glanced across at him. 'I'm not sure what she can do.'

'She's the district councillor, Martin,' Phil scoffed. 'Surely she has some say.'

'She can make a comment…' Martin began.

'We should write a letter to the *Sudleigh Gazette*,' Clive stated.

Lydia raised an eyebrow and sipped her Pinot Noir.

'We just want as many people as possible to post objections online,' Martin said.

'What about a leaflet drop?' Phil rubbed his paunch.

'Absolutely,' Clive agreed, nodding.

'And we need to demolish them at the planning committee,' Phil advised.

'Who'll be spokesman?' Susan asked.

'I think Martin should do it,' Clive said. 'You're good at that sort of thing.'

'Agreed,' Phil said.

'I really don't think…' Martin gripped the edge of the table.

'Show of hands everyone?' Jacqui hinged forward, scanned the faces.

'Look, I'd rather not get…' Martin complained.

'All those in favour of Martin presenting the argument?' Jacqui proposed.

Martin massaged his forehead, forced a smile.

'So that's decided then,' Hugh said, reaching for his glass.

'How was Dubai, Susan?' Lydia quietly asked.

★

It was freezing hard now, the pavement glittered with frost. He walked slowly homeward; he only lived a few doors away. Beside him tall hedges rose up, screening the set-back houses. The sharp air carried the musty tang of coal smoke. This was his road; it was where he'd put down roots, brought up a family. He stared ahead; two hundred yards further on, the road veered off at a right angle and the streetlights ceased. There was darkness beyond, where the fields took over from the town and rolled up the black hillside. No, they had to fight this development; it would change everything.

He unwound his scarf and threw it onto the coat stand. Bridget's hairdryer was whining upstairs, muted behind the bedroom door. Unzipping his jacket, he ambled along the hallway, passing the photographs on the wall, their daughters, Emily and Virginia, from gap-toothed primary school grins to mortar-boarded graduations. He drifted into the dining room, draped his coat over the back of a chair. His laptop was on the table, open, waiting. He slid his finger across the mousepad and sat, squinting at the glare as the screen revived. There was a new email. He read it quickly, then typed a reply.

'Not sure we can call a paint shade 'Gypsy Blush.' 'Dusted Fudge' and 'Brumous Dawn' are good. More the tone. We're presenting ideas on Monday. Tell them if they haven't made significant progress by tomorrow lunchtime, they'll be sacked.'

A new account had come in, rebranding a paint manufacturer, sexing it up. The young copywriters weren't taking it seriously; but he'd been the same, fresh out of Oxford with his geography degree, all those years ago.

He pushed his glasses up his forehead and pinched the bridge of his nose. Grey growth had overrun his once dark hair; there were pouchy, blue-black shadows beneath his eyes. Slumping back, he gazed idly at the screen and thought about his commute back from London.

The train had been delayed, hung up outside Surbiton. It was packed; people coughing, talking into phones, the smell of burger grease lingering in the air. A woman had crammed onto the seat beside him, elbowing him each time she turned the page of her *Metro*.

'…incident on the line ahead…waiting for the police…' the guard had announced. Everyone knew what that meant. A suicide.

'I'm supposed to be meeting friends for a meal,' the woman complained. Thankfully her phone had rung.

'You're back,' Bridget said, slippering past the doorway. He heard her in the kitchen, the fridge door opening and closing again.

'Mmm.'

'How was the meeting?' She scuffed into the room, rested her thigh against the table and folded her arms, cradling a bottle of water. She was wearing the white towelling robe he'd bought her for Christmas.

'I thought you didn't want to know.'

She pulled her robe closed at the throat. 'What are they going to do?'

'A leaflet drop, apparently. I think this is Phil's Vietnam.'

She laughed. 'What else?'

'Oh, the usual. Objections on the website.'

Bridget pressed her lips together.

Martin reached up, stroked her arm. 'There is one thing though…' He hesitated, withdrew his hand. 'I don't think you're going to like it.'

'What is it?'

He flicked her a glance. 'They want me to be spokesman.'

She inhaled sharply, expelled a loud sigh. 'You did say no, didn't you?'

He hunched his shoulders. 'I didn't feel I could.'

'I thought we'd agreed.' She was searching his eyes.

Creases ridged his forehead. 'Do you really want a housing estate at the top of the road?'

She shook her head and walked away, then turned back. 'We did talk about this, Martin.'

'You talked about this,' Martin protested, but she'd gone before he finished.

He gazed vacantly at the computer screen, listening to the

dull creak as Bridget climbed the stairs. The screen's brightness was making his eyes ache. He removed his glasses, slid them onto the table, then rubbed his face with both hands. She was different now. It had begun a while ago. He stared myopically into the corner of the room. Once the girls had left, she'd started networking, schmoozing down at the Conservative Club, at the Rotary Club, 'getting involved'. When a vacancy on the District Council had arisen, she'd been nominated. Then, once she'd been selected, she started taking it seriously. 'I want to make a difference,' she'd told him. 'I want to do something that matters.' She'd actually said that. And now, nine months later, she was willing to let developers build a housing estate on their doorstep.

Martin gripped the back of his neck. Somewhere, behind his eyes he could feel a headache building, pushing forward to a point.

*

On Saturday morning, just after nine, Martin was clattering along the hallway. The plastic bases of his cycling shoes clacked on the hardwood floor. He stopped by the front door, lifted his cycling helmet from the coat stand, patted it on then clicked the clasp shut under his chin. He looked up; Bridget was carrying a bundle of washing down the stairs. She didn't acknowledge him.

Watching her walk through to the kitchen, he bent his

knees slightly, reached down and plucked at his Lycra cycling shorts, repositioning a grating seam. He'd hardly seen her yesterday; he'd had a late meeting at work, savaging the copywriters. And she'd been out early with her horse this morning.

'What have you got on today?' he called, tottering after her.

She leaned her head out from the utility room. 'I wish you wouldn't walk through the house in those, Martin.' She disappeared again; the washing machine door clicked shut.

He surveyed the kitchen: the polished granite worksurfaces, the breakfast bar, the brushed-steel stove with suspended extractor cowl. It had all been new six months ago.

'Isn't there something civic?'

'Re-opening the community centre café?' she called.

'Mmm...' Out through the kitchen window, there was a thick mist hazing the garden, obscuring the fence down at the end.

'That was yesterday.' The washing machine was already filling as Bridget moved out into the kitchen. She stalled. 'Have you decided what you're doing about this campaign?'

'What campaign?'

'Fight for Sudleigh.'

Martin plucked at his shorts again. 'Come on, Bridget. You know I can't just let it happen. It'll change everything.'

She was walking towards him, shaking her head. 'Change has to happen sometime.' She brushed past him, swept into the hallway. 'It's how things stay alive.'

He sensed that, somehow, she wasn't actually talking about the housing estate. She paused at the bottom of the stairs, one foot on a low step. He teetered towards her.

'I'm asking you not to get involved,' she said.

'Will you stop going on about it?' he said, advancing. 'I only asked what you're doing this afternoon.'

'Going out with Ginny.' She began her ascent. 'And I'll stop going on about it when you stop being so selfish.'

Martin lurched towards the door.

Outside, the grey mist scarcely stirred. The branches overhanging the driveway were rime-coated; the spiders' webs on the conifer hedge had thickened, crystallised. Martin stepped across to the garage. He stooped and unlocked the door, then raised it, the steel springs twanging. How could she call him selfish? He wheeled the bike onto the driveway, propped it against his hip and pulled down the garage door. For a moment he gazed down through the thin cloud of his sinking breath. She was the one being unreasonable.

He walked his bike to the end of the driveway, mounted stiffly then bobbled out across the root-cracked pavement and onto the road. Accelerating, he passed the detached houses, half-hidden behind their silvered hedges. He rounded the bend at the top of the road, and settled into an easy, rolling rhythm. He looked right, across the doomed field. It was already staked in preparation; the hedgerows ripped out. How could they build all those houses here? It wouldn't be the same any more. It would shift the boundaries. He had to fight it. What choice did he have? Bridget would understand.

At the junction, he heaved onto the narrow country road, then pushed beyond the town's farthest reach. Beneath the threadbare arch of naked branches, he wound up the long hill. The golf club slipped past, its car park full, and on he pressed, out into the country.

Martin kicked off his shoes. He was sweating torrentially; his legs felt alien, like they were someone else's. As he hobbled towards the kitchen, he heard Bridget's voice. 'You're absolutely right...' Was she on the phone?

There was a man by the breakfast bar; Bridget was standing over by the kettle in the corner.

'Hello, Martin,' Brian said.

Brian was the longest-serving town councillor. Martin had met him a few times at the Conservative Club during Bridget's election campaign.

'Brian,' Martin said, approaching the sink. He picked a glass from the draining board, filled it under the tap, then gulped down the water and turned.

Bridget stared across at him. 'Brian was just saying how development is a good thing.'

'Was he?' Martin dragged his wrist across his mouth. He studied Brian briefly; the sparse slicked-back hair, the pencil-thin moustache. Awful man.

'It lets young people get on the housing ladder, brings people into the town...' Brian raised his mug, swilled back the last of its contents and thoughtfully puckered his lips.

Martin watched the loose flesh swing under Brian's chin. A wattle, he decided.

'There are lots of benefits,' Bridget said, widening her eyes at Martin.

'I'm not sure the people round here would agree.'

Bridget shook her head at him.

Brian sniffed. 'You see, Martin, you've got to look at the bigger picture.'

'Ah, the bigger picture.' He didn't need a lecture from this man.

'The developers are going to contribute a million pounds to the council's coffers.'

Martin pulled a face at Bridget but she ignored him.

'It's a goodwill gesture,' Brian explained. 'And that money can do a lot of good.'

Bridget nodded enthusiastically. 'It would make a huge difference, Brian.'

'Sounds like a bung to me,' Martin said. Bridget was glaring at him.

'It'll go a long way towards refurbishing the Sports Centre,' Brian continued. 'And it'll re-roof the Scout Hut. The whole town'll benefit.'

'Will it?' Martin scoffed.

'Anyway,' Brian said, fingering back his sleeve, checking his watch, 'I should go. I only called in to see how you're getting on.' He placed his cup on the breakfast bar. 'I'm supposed to be teeing off at twelve.'

'Thanks so much for coming, Brian.' Bridget breezed towards him.

'Brian,' Martin said flatly.

Bridget followed Brian into the hall. 'I think it's so important that we work…'

'Christ,' Martin muttered as he turned and refilled his glass. He drank then skidded the empty glass across the worktop. Outside, the mist had thickened.

'What were you thinking,' Bridget said, 'calling it a bung?'

He turned, shrugged at her. 'It's what it sounded like.'

'Do you know how influential he is?' She collected Brian's cup as she crossed the kitchen.

'He's a pig farmer.'

Bridget paused over by the kettle, gathered her cup. 'You really are a snob, aren't you?'

'I don't know why you let him in the house.' Martin retreated a couple of steps, rested his hip against the dishwasher.

She moved towards the sink. 'Because he's worried you're going to sabotage this development.'

'It's an objection,' Martin corrected.

'Have you any idea how you're making me look?'

He smiled. The drying sweat was gummy in the creases of his skin.

She deposited the mugs in the washing up bowl. 'Like I'm married to an idiot.'

Martin snorted. 'I'm hardly an idiot.'

'Well, you're acting like one.' She pivoted towards him, planted her hands on her hips.

He leaned his elbow onto the cool stone worktop. 'Did you invite him?'

She pointed towards the hallway. 'He came to find out which side I'm on.' Her voice had risen now.

'Ah, laying down the party line.' Martin barked a derisive laugh.

'No.'

'I mean, do you actually believe all that bullshit?'

Someone was knocking at the front door, the sound hollowing as it echoed along the hallway.

'It made perfect sense to me,' she said, setting off across the kitchen.

'Jesus, Bridget. Have you listened to yourself lately?' he called after her.

He heard the front door open, heard the voice. 'Sorry I'm late, Mum.' It was Virginia, their younger daughter. He stood straight then waded, stiff-legged, across the room.

'Come in a second,' Bridget said. The front door closed.

Martin arrived in the kitchen doorway. 'Hello, Ginny.'

Virginia was tall, blond, had her mother's features. She walked towards him then stopped short. 'Good god, Dad,' she said, surveying him. 'What are you wearing?' Behind her, Bridget perched on a low stair.

'Been out on the bike.'

'You should talk to him about this, Mum,' Ginny said,

laughing.

Bridget was hauling on a boot. 'Unfortunately, your father doesn't listen to my opinions any more, Ginny.'

'Not when she wants ninety houses at the top of the road.'

'Are you two arguing?' Ginny asked, glancing back at Bridget.

'Just a little dispute about my right to protest,' Martin explained.

Bridget pulled on her other boot. 'Don't drag Virginia into this.' She stood and yanked her jacket from the coat stand.

'So, where are you two going?' he asked, changing the subject.

'Fitting for my wedding dress,' Ginny said. 'And going for lunch after. Come if you want.'

Bridget pushed her arm into her coat. 'I'm sure your dad's far too busy.'

'I'd love to, but...' Martin began.

'Right,' Bridget said, wrenching the door open. 'Are we ready?'

Virginia stepped forward and kissed Martin lightly on the cheek. 'You're very sticky, Dad.' She stepped back and looked him over again, grinning. 'I'm surprised you've got the nerve to go out like that.'

He tracked her along the hall. 'Drive carefully,' he said, as she crossed the threshold. Bridget was already outside, striding towards the Range Rover parked across the end of the driveway. He watched her for a moment, the chill air wrapping around him, then he closed the door.

Once he'd showered, Martin settled to work.

He was sitting at the dining-room table, the laptop in front of him. A grey, muffled light was leaking in through the window. The mist hadn't lifted all day.

He stared at the screen. Was 'Bruised Mint' actually suitable? And was 'Bruised Mint' really any different from 'Almost Jade 4'? He looked out through the window. Bridget wasn't back yet. What was happening to her? He used to know how she thought; he'd understood her. She would never have tolerated someone like Brian Nash in the past. And she'd become argumentative. She was changing. It was all changing, somehow.

★

He took a bite of his cheese on toast, wiped the grease from his fingers onto the leg of his tracksuit bottoms, then typed.

'…the paint range becomes part of a lifestyle choice. It makes your brand vibrant, reaching out to millennials and those in middle-age who want to stay on-trend. The names are an extension of…' What were they an extension of?

There was a diffuse red flare at the top of the drive, a car door slammed. He took another bite of cheese on toast, pushed the crust into his mouth. The car blipped its horn as it pulled away. A key grated in the lock; the door opened; closed.

He leaned back. 'How did it go?' As he spoke, a morsel of cheese shot from his mouth, landed on the table. He pinched it up, sucked it from his finger. He stood, wandered into the hallway. Bridget was already at the top of the stairs.

'How was the fitting, Bridget?' he called.

Taps were being cranked; water was rattling in the bath. Martin ascended.

He stood in the doorway of the bathroom. She was bending, pushing the plug into its hole, then she reached for the decanter of bath foam and poured some into the water. The sound of running water reverberated around the tiled walls, steam billowed, the lime scent rising.

'Is something wrong?' he asked.

She re-stoppered the decanter, replaced it, then wheeled to face him. 'Apparently, my beliefs are bullshit.'

Martin laughed nervously. 'I didn't actually say that.'

'It's what you implied.'

'I didn't mean it like that.' He stepped forward, draped an arm across her shoulders. 'Sorry, Bridget. It was…'

She writhed free and exited the bathroom. He followed her through to the bedroom. She was facing the long mirror on the wardrobe, pulling off her sweater.

'What's really going on?' he asked, softly.

She shook her head at his reflection and began unbuttoning her shirt. 'I asked you not to get involved with this Fight for Sudleigh thing. You know what this place is like.'

'What are you talking about?'

'Brian must have heard something. He was checking up on me.'

'So?' Martin flared his nostrils dismissively.

She snapped round, her shirt hanging open. 'You're making me look stupid.'

'Are you sure you want to be involved in this local politics stuff?'

'This is important to me, Martin.' She peeled off her shirt, threw it at the wicker basket in the corner.

'But people like Brian are dangerous. They drag you in, compromise you.'

'What is it you don't understand? It's a job I actually want to do. It means something.' She unfastened the top button of her trousers.

'I wouldn't call it a job, Bridget,' he sneered.

She released a strange strangled scream, then rushed towards him, barged past. The bathroom door slammed.

He rocked back his head, stared at the ceiling briefly, then trudged out of the room and across the landing. 'I didn't mean it like that,' he said, easing open the bathroom door.

She'd taken off her trousers, was bending over the bath, stirring the water with a hand.

'You don't really want all those houses at the top of the road, do you?'

Straightening, she reached behind her, unfastened her bra and removed it, then dropped it onto the toilet lid. 'This isn't just about houses,' she said, sliding down her briefs.

'Of course it is.'

She shook her head at him then turned away. 'I think you need to work out what this is really about.' She lifted a foot over the edge of the bath, sank it into the water. 'You need to make a choice.' Leaning a hand on the wall, she raised her other foot.

'What choice? You're not making any sense.'

She squatted down into the water then, holding onto the bath's sides, lowered herself into the foam. 'Work it out, Martin.' She bent forward, cranked off the taps, then settled back.

'But it'll ruin the neighbourhood.'

She slid down into the suds, her flesh skidding across the bottom of the bath.

'Come on, Bridget. Can't we even talk about this?'

'What else is there to say?' She wiggled her toes.

'I don't see why I'm the bad guy.'

She slipped down and submerged her head beneath the water.

'You're being impossible,' he said, but she didn't resurface. He slammed the door behind him and stood for a moment on the landing. 'Fucking ridiculous,' he shouted, hoping Bridget could hear.

The next day, Martin was sitting at the dinner table. He was trying to develop the social media pitch, but found himself, instead, staring out of the window, watching the thickening fog. He'd tried to talk to her again this morning when she came back from the stables.

'I'm sorry if I've upset you...'

She hadn't even looked at him; she'd just carried her riding boots through to the utility room.

He'd stood in the doorway. 'You know I completely support you with this district councillor thing...' She'd pushed past him, crossed the kitchen. 'But it's ninety houses,' he'd said towards her receding back.

He'd hurried through to the hallway as she climbed the stairs. 'Can't we even have a civilised conversation, now?' he called.

The bedroom door had clicked shut.

Martin looked at the computer screen. If this carried on, he'd sleep in one of the girls' old rooms tonight. He slouched back in his chair. For some reason, he thought about the suicide on the train the other day, the sudden sharp impact, the choice. He shuddered, rolled his shoulders then tried to reread the last unfinished sentence. But his mind wouldn't fix on it. Was that what it was, the suicide? A protest against the impossibility of it all? He couldn't think about that.

He tried to force his mind back to the social media campaign.

He returned home late on the Monday evening. He had another headache building, deep behind his eyes. He hadn't slept well the night before, in the unfamiliar bed.

He closed the front door behind him and trailed the smell of cooking into the kitchen. Bridget was placing her plate in the dishwasher.

'I've left you some sauce in the pan,' she said. 'You'll have to do your own pasta.' She crossed the kitchen, walked past him and out into the hallway, her head bowed, her eyes down.

He raised a hand and massaged his forehead. 'How long is this…' he started, but fell silent. As he walked across to the hob, he heard the front door shut. He stepped into the middle of the kitchen, rested his palms on the cool granite work surface of the breakfast bar and hung his head.

★

'You look tired, Martin,' Dr Hugh said.

Thursday had come round again. The Fight for Sudleigh group had re-convened.

'Not sleeping, Hugh.' Martin smiled faintly, the creases round his eyes deeper than usual, the bags beneath a purplish-black.

'So does everyone know what to put in their objections?' Phil checked.

There were murmurs.

'Now, I've put this leaflet together,' he went on. 'I think it's essential we mobilise the whole neighbourhood.' He passed copies of the leaflet around.

Martin left his copy flat on the table, untouched.

'The more of us there are, the stronger our voice,' Phil said. Martin glanced across at him. There was a manic fervour about Phil, the way he was staring and prodding the table. 'We need a coordinated resistance.'

Martin lowered his head and pinched the bridge of his nose.

'It's very good, Phil,' Susan said. 'But isn't it a little strong?'

'I don't think we should call them 'corrupt butchers of community,' Hugh said.

'But I've printed them now. They were 5p a copy.'

'I'm just not entirely sure I'm happy being connected to this,' Hugh said.

Martin looked around the group. He drew a deep breath, released it. 'Are we even sure that the development is such a bad thing?' he said, slowly, regretfully.

There was a cool silence.

'I mean,' he pressed on, 'people have to live somewhere, don't they?'

'What are you saying, Martin?' Phil asked.

'It's just that, perhaps, we have to accept that progress is going to happen.'

'This is Bridget talking, isn't it?' Phil said.

'Really,' Dr Hugh interjected mildly. 'I don't think there's any need for that.'

'Well?' Phil insisted, glaring across the table.

'No, it's not Bridget. It's just that, you know, the town's got to grow, hasn't it? Should we stand in the way of that?'

'Of course we should. I've never heard such nonsense.' Phil threw a hand in the air, landed it heavily on the table.

'Watch the wine, Phil,' Jacqui said.

Lydia was half-smiling, uncertain, looking from face to face.

'They're going to build houses, whether we like it or not,' Martin said.

'Motion to rescind Martin's election as representative at the planning meeting,' Phil said loudly, slapping the table.

'There's no need to be such an arse, Phil,' Clive said.

A squabble broke out.

Beneath the table, Jacqui placed a hand on Martin's sleeve. 'Is everything OK, Martin?'

Martin smiled sadly, hung his head. 'I'm just tired.'

Bridget was snoring beside him. It was more a low snuffle than a full, rasping snore. Martin lay on his back, staring up at the wedge of amber light across the ceiling that crept in through a crack in the curtains. He twisted his neck and looked at the alarm clock. The red-lit numbers told 3.15. He had to be up in less than four hours. He was replaying the meeting in his mind. Phil had cut up nasty.

'You're an absolute charlatan,' he'd said.

A snore caught in Bridget's throat. As though accidentally, Martin kicked her leg. She shifted, groaned, fell quiet. He traced a crack in the ceiling, buried beneath the wallpaper.

And tonight she'd started on about having the bedrooms re-carpeted. But he'd put a stop to that; he had to draw the line somewhere. Rolling on to his side, he punched a fresh dent into his pillow and lowered his head. The alarm clock told 3.22 already.

FRANK & TED

1990

Sleet slapped against the windscreen, the wiper-blades squealed. Warm stale air was gusting in through the van's vents.

'I've never known anything like it,' Frank said. He drew hard on his cigarette, a column of ash falling. 'We had them with that rhumba.'

From the passenger seat, Ted quietly watched the curtain-drawn houses slide by.

Frank carelessly brushed at his lap. 'I mean, asking us to call the bingo numbers in the middle of a set.' He laughed, shook his head.

'I thought you did it quite professionally,' Ted said, smiling. He gazed at the road ahead, the streetlights reflecting dully from the slicked tarmac.

'Furore' they were called; an organ duo. They'd started out playing lounges, functions, tea dances, but the work had dried up. Now they were playing working men's clubs; it had been Swindon tonight.

Another run of sleeping houses slipped past. Frank steered the corner where the pebble-dashed police station loitered, then wound down the window. He sucked a last drag on his cigarette, pushed the butt out through the gap and cranked up the window. 'Frightening thing is, they said they'd have us back anytime.'

Ted cleared his throat. 'About that, Frank...'

Frank swung the van round a bend, accelerated.

'I've been meaning to, er...' Ted ran his tongue across his lips, inhaled sharply. 'Look, Frank, I can't keep doing this.'

'How d'you mean?' Frank glanced across.

'Well...' Ted gripped his knees. 'I've been offered a job on a cruise ship.'

'A cruise ship?' Frank fumbled in his jacket pocket, pulled out a cigarette packet, flipped it open against his chin. 'Doing what?'

Ted stared straight ahead. 'I went for an audition. Pianist and organist.'

Frank drew out a cigarette with his teeth, dropped the packet back into his pocket. He looked across at Ted, then faced forward. 'What about the bookings?' he asked, the cigarette waggling. 'You're letting people down.'

'Don't be like that, Frank.'

'Like what?'

Ted pushed his glasses up his nose. 'Look at it. If Gill's pregnant, you can't start clearing off on the cruise ships for six months, can you?'

'That's not the point though, is it?' Frank shook his head then braked hard and swerved onto a side street. 'How long have you known?'

'I've got to think about my career…'

'What career?' Frank laughed sourly. The van slowed; its tyre scuffed the kerb outside Ted's flat, the ground floor of a red-brick terrace. He cut the engine; the heater fell silent. 'I should have known you'd do something like this.'

Ted turned down the corners of his mouth, shrugged.

Leaning back against the door, Frank thumbed the lighter. The flame threw a wavering glow over his stubbled face. He sucked at the filter tip, the tobacco crisply crackling. The exhaled smoke roiled against the windscreen. 'You should've told me, Ted.'

Drips from the skeletal tree branches overhead drummed on the roof; the engine ticked as it cooled. Frank dragged on his cigarette.

'I'll get my stuff out,' Ted said quietly. He wrenched the handle, let the door fall open with the road's camber then stepped down from the van.

He walked round, opened the rear door and dragged his amplifier towards him. After depositing it in his hallway, he hurried back to the van. Shivering, dipping his head into the slanting sleet, he lifted out his keyboard, then, balancing it on his thigh, he slammed the door shut. As he scuttered along the path to his flat, he heard the engine start, rev hard. He turned and watched Frank drive away, the tail lights receding.

2019

Once Ted had checked into the hotel, he decided to take a walk. It had been a long drive from Lincolnshire.

He stopped outside the Boots store, looking back along the high street. The gusting wind lifted his tie. All the old shops had gone, Woolworths and the rest. Now there were coffee shops, pound shops, charity shops. It had changed, deteriorated. Drawing a deep breath he noticed the absence of the sour tang which used to drift across town from the brewery. It had closed a couple of years ago; he'd read that somewhere.

He crossed the road, made his way down Lower Turk Street, a narrow one-way abbreviated by a mini-roundabout. At the junction, he slowed, surveying the Sainsbury's opposite. It was new, to his knowledge, but it already looked worn. He checked his watch: 4.45. He needed to get back to the hotel and eat before the evening's show. He quickened his pace then, abruptly, halted.

There was a blockish concrete building set back from the pavement. The sign over the door announced 'Watson's Carpets' in tall, blue lettering. Could that be the Watson he used to know? Frank Watson? Could he really still be in town after all these years?

The door groaned closed behind him. There were indistinct voices emanating from somewhere down at the far end of the showroom. He meandered along an aisle, studying the wool twist and easy-clean displays, roll on roll, rack after rack. At the end of the aisle, he stalled. There was a middle-aged couple standing at the counter. The man on the business side was prodding a calculator.

'For both bedrooms it should be nine-seven-five,' the man looked up at the customers, 'but, since it's you Bridget, we can do it for eight-fifty.'

Ted's stomach flipped. It was; it was Frank. The black hair of Frank's youth had been shaded grey; his jowls hung slack; his shoulders were slightly more sloped, but it was definitely Frank. Suddenly, Ted could feel the sweat starting in his hair. Why had he come in? What would he say? He began to pat his pockets, first his jacket, then his trousers. He took a step backwards, and another, then tapped his forehead and tutted, as though remembering that he'd left something crucial in the car. Turning, he walked quickly along the aisle, then out through the door.

He looked back at the shop from the pavement. Watson's Carpets. He tugged the lapels of his jacket, then, with a forward jut of his chin, straightened his tie.

Ted sat at a table by the window, waiting for his meal to arrive. There were three or four middle-aged couples dotted around the dining room of the old Georgian coaching house. A group of suited business-types bantered by the bar, one of them yelping at a slot machine.

He watched the after-work people, the college kids pass outside. He reached for his glass of iced water, sipped. Strange, he thought, how the place had changed, but it was still the same sleepy backwater he'd once known. And yet, somehow, it felt like he'd never lived here; like those times had never happened.

A passing bus blocked the light for a moment, caused the water in his glass to ripple. Odd seeing Frank again…

There was movement at the table beside him.

'You sit on that side, Gordon,' a woman said.

Chairs were being dragged out. It was a couple, retirement age. The man caught Ted's eye.

'Howdo?' he said with a wink and a twitch of his head.

Northerners, Ted decided. He smiled pleasantly, the fine creases crinkling beside his eyes.

'Lovely little place this, isn't it?' the woman said, smoothing out the skirt under her legs before she sat.

'You staying here as well?' the man asked, unfastening his jacket, tilting his head towards the bar.

'Just the night. Passing through.'

The man nodded. 'Here for our son's wedding.' He leaned back, his paunch straining his shirt buttons. 'Thought we'd make a little holiday of it.'

'That sounds nice.' Ted had learned, over the years, to give the right responses. People seemed to talk to him, to tell him their stories.

'You from round here?' the man asked.

Ted smiled. 'I used to be. Just back on business.'

'Gordon used to travel all the time for work, didn't you, Gordon?'

'Spent my life in airports,' Gordon said, tucking the loosened shirt flap back into his trousers.

'Missed the children growing up, didn't you?' the woman said, matter-of-factly.

'Well, someone had to pay the school fees,' he replied drily.

Ted's gaze strayed out of the window. No, he wasn't missing anything, being single, being free.

'Stuart's an accountant up in London,' the woman stated.

Ted looked at her, inquiringly.

'Our son,' the man said, cocking his head towards his wife, rolling his eyes apologetically.

She scowled at Gordon.

A double act, Ted decided.

'Done very nicely for himself,' she continued.

'Very nicely,' Gordon confirmed.

'Hunter's Chicken?' Ted hadn't heard the waiter approach. He glanced up, thankful of the intrusion.

'That's me,' he said, sliding his glass towards the centre of the table, swaying to a side.

'Would you like any sauces with that, sir?'

'No, I'm fine, thanks.' Ted smiled up at the young waiter,

eyed the name badge. 'Thank you, Tom. This looks great.'

'So polite down here, aren't they?' the woman commented as the waiter retreated.

Ted nodded, took hold of his knife and fork.

'And his wife-to-be's lovely,' said the woman, dipping back into her previous stream. 'You should see where they're having the wedding…'

The fluorescent bulb over the sink flickered on. Ted looked into the mirror, lifted his chin, twisted his bow tie straight. Leaning towards the glass, he examined his moustache, noticed a few stray bristles. Reaching down, he unzipped the toiletries bag behind the taps and delved until he felt the cool steel of his scissors. With deft, bonsai-precision, he snipped away the offending filaments, then, tilting back his head, he clipped away a rogue nasal hair.

He dropped the scissors back into the bag, then touched a hand to the flashes of grey at his temple, ran his fingers through his sandy hair. Life had been kind, he knew. A decade on the cruise ships; then working in America for Roland Keyboards in development and design, and later touring Europe as marketing specialist/artist. He'd returned to England three years ago, to take it easy, to do what he loved, to play to audiences again. He couldn't have envisaged any of that when he left town all those years ago.

The sun had long dipped below the roofs of the buildings across the street. The darkness in his room had thickened. He walked across, pressed the light-switch, then unzipped the suit-bag hanging from the hook on the door.

With one arm in the sleeve of his white dinner jacket, he paused, surveying the open bag on the bed, the small kettle on the table, the ramekin of sachets beside it. He'd never known what he wanted when he was younger. But he couldn't have settled; would never have been happy just staying in the same place, selling carpets. He pushed his other arm into the sleeve. No, he'd been right to leave; he'd made the right choices. He stooped, pulled on his shoes, then, sitting on the edge of the bed, bent to fasten his laces.

The Sudleigh Organ and Keyboard Club met once a month at the Grange Hotel, a low-slung building on the fringe of town. Ted had already set up his equipment on the stage at the far end of the conference room.

He was sitting behind his two-tiered keyboard. The PA speakers hissed slightly. Without looking down he pressed the button. The rhythm began, a swinging Bossa Nova. That was the thing about these gigs, Ted reflected, the people were always so appreciative. They were easy audiences.

He glanced out at the empty tables which extended up the room. He flicked his hands forward so his sleeves retreated above his wrist, then lowered his fingers to the keyboard and began a Latin-flavoured rendition of 'A Whiter Shade Of Pale.' His movements were expert, minimal, his head pecked time, his feet skipped, toe and heeling across the bass pedals.

Absorbed in the moment, he allowed the music to flow.

After two verses he lifted his hands from the keyboard, reached forward and stopped the beat. The PA's hiss filled the silence.

'How was that, Alan?' he called.

Alan Dawson, chairman of the Sudleigh Organ and Keyboard Club advanced from the rear of the room. 'Sounded great,' he said, approaching the stage. He was a spry, well-tanned man, white-haired, dapper. He was smiling broadly, rubbing his hands together.

'Not too loud?' Ted pulled his sleeves down.

'No, perfect. Superb accordion setting that. And the rhythms…'

Ted stood. 'Fantastic bit of kit, this, the Roland Atelier AT-900.'

'It certainly is,' Alan agreed, nodding.

Ted walked to the front of the stage. 'A bargain for what they can do.'

A handful of people were ambling up the room, chatting, laughing.

'Oh, I meant to ask,' Alan said. 'Do you need a microphone stand?'

For an instant, Ted's eyes became glassy, unseeing. He'd been working on the cruise ships. It must have been a Valentine's Day. They were rolling in heavy seas. Someone had requested 'Je T'Aime.' That was the last time he'd tried his falsetto in public; the last time he'd sung in anger. A smile creased Ted's face; there had been some memorable moments on the cruise ships. He looked back at Alan, then stepped down onto the parquet dance floor. 'No, I'll be fine. I'll just talk into the hand-held, and leave it on top of the Atelier when I'm playing.'

'Great,' Alan said. The first arrivals were taking their seats. He touched Ted's elbow. 'I'm going to have to talk to a few people.'

Ted moved across the front of the stage, to the shadowy corner by the fire door, watching as more people filtered in. It was going to be a good turnout; fifty or sixty Alan had predicted earlier. The room was filling. He smoothed his moustache as he felt the familiar twist in his gut. He loved this waiting period, the nervous excitement. It had never lost its thrill.

After a while, Alan mounted the steps at the side of the stage. He picked the microphone from the top of Ted's keyboard.

'Hello everybody. Nice to see you all again. And welcome to a couple of new faces. We'll be following the usual format tonight. First off, the stage is open to anyone who wants to get up and play, to show us what they've been working on. You can use the Club's organ.' He paused, as though retracing rehearsed lines. 'Personally, I'm very excited about Alice's new disco styling of "You Really Got Me." That should set things off with a swing.' There were murmurings among the crowd. Someone chortled, at a private joke. 'And then our guest performer… Where are you, Ted?'

Ted stepped forward, held up a hand, mouthed 'Hello

everyone.'

'Ted'll give us a set and then talk to us about his career in music, on the high seas and working for Roland in America, in...' Alan hesitated, 'design and development and touring Europe. Is that right, Ted?'

Ted smiled professionally, nodded. He stepped back into the shadows, adjusted his tie.

Ted checked out of the hotel ten minutes before the eleven o'clock deadline. Once he'd dumped his bags on the back seat of his Mercedes, he drove the short distance to the car park in front of Watson's Carpets.

He stood beside his car, the wind snapping at his slacks, and thumbed the button on his key fob. The sidelights blinked, the central locking clunked. There was nervousness flitting in his stomach, like before a show.

Inside the shop, he threaded along an aisle, browsing the Berber, Axminster and Wilton possibilities. The smell of carpets, new and untrodden, filled his nostrils, made him want to sneeze.

Frank was at the counter again, alone, his head bowed, punching something into the computer with heavy prods of his index fingers.

Ted's throat tightened; he felt slightly sick. He wasn't sure he could do this. He spun round, spied a fat book of carpet swatches propped on a melamined pedestal. He moved across to it, keeping his back to Frank, and flipped the heavy pages.

Should he just go? Maybe that would be best. He ran his fingers through a deep velvet plush, watching the darker track marks left behind. Must be a swine to vacuum.

'Are you OK there?' the voice at his shoulder enquired.

Ted's stomach dropped; he swallowed hard, turned. He saw the recognition kindle in Frank's eyes. He scanned Frank's face; the creases round his eyes, beside his nose, were deeply scored, his stubble ineradicably dense.

Ted cleared his throat. 'Hello, Frank.'

'I thought it was you.'

'How are you?' Ted ran a finger under his collar.

Frank folded his arms. He was wearing a Golf Club V-neck under his jacket. 'Oh, surviving.'

Ted's gaze wandered as he searched for something to say.

'And you?' Frank asked.

Ted raised his shoulders. 'Oh, not too bad, thanks. Getting by.'

'So what brings you to these parts?'

'Oh, just a thing with the Keyboard Club.'

Frank rocked back his head, snorted a laugh. 'You're not still doing that, are you?'

Ted smiled. Frank was still the same.

'Well,' Ted said brightly, 'you've certainly got a lot of carpets.'

'Everything you could want. And if we don't have it, we can get it.'

Ted grinned at the patter. The telephone was ringing.

'Alright then, nice to see you, Ted.' Frank was backing

away, holding up a hand in farewell. 'Bye,' he said, then jogged towards the counter, lifted the handset to his ear.

Ted revisited the book of swatches, flipped the pages.

'Hello, Watson's Carpets,' he heard Frank say. 'Oh, hello again, Miss Bennett... What size is the room?...We could send someone round to measure up for you... How's ten o'clock tomorrow?... In the morning... All right, I'll put that in the book then... Ten am... All right, yep. Bye Miss Bennett.'

Ted closed the swatch book and advanced towards the counter. Frank was writing something in a large diary. Then he dragged the mouse, double-clicked and began poking the keyboard.

Ted stood quietly, contemplating a display of carpet tiles.

After a while, Frank stopped typing, looked up. 'What did you actually want, Ted?'

Ted smiled back at him, surprised. 'I just thought I could buy you a coffee, catch up. You know?'

Frank's thick eyebrows arched. 'I can't just shut the shop. Trevor's out measuring up and Gill's got the grandkids.'

'Well, I just wanted to say hello, really. See how you're doing. It's been a long time, Frank.' Frank was staring at him. 'And I don't know if I'll be passing through again.' Ted pressed his lips together, shrugged poignantly.

Frank's shoulders sagged. 'Right,' he said, releasing a long, low sigh. He dragged an invoice towards him, peered at the computer screen and began to type.

'So...' Ted began, 'it's changed a bit round here, hasn't it?'

'Well, they keep building more houses.' Frank didn't raise his head.

Ted noticed the light dusting of dandruff on Frank's collar. 'It's the same everywhere,' he concurred.

'Worked out well for us, business-wise.' Frank continued to type.

Ted rocked up onto his toes, sank again. 'So how's the family? How's Gill?' He knew Gill had never really liked him.

Frank's face softened. 'Oh, she's all right,' he said. 'Snowed under with the grandkids, but she loves it.'

'Grandkids,' Ted said warmly. 'How many?'

Frank stood upright. 'Two, at the moment. Daniel's. I don't think he'd been born when you left.' There was a glow to Frank now. 'And our Laura's expecting.'

'That's wonderful, Frank. They're spawning.'

Frank laughed slightly as he reached into the inside pocket of his jacket and extracted a battered brown leather wallet. He pulled out a photograph and passed it across to Ted.

'That's them.'

A boy and girl. They looked happy, full of mischief. 'You must be very proud, Frank,' Ted said, returning the photograph.

Frank smiled as he eased the picture back into his wallet, then dropped the wallet into his pocket.

'So, what about you?' Frank asked. 'Ever marry?'

Ted laughed slightly. 'No. Never met the right person.'

'Still a bachelor, eh?'

Ted lowered his eyes.

'So where did you get to? Did you ever find what you were looking for?'

'I saw the world on the cruise ships.'

'I heard you were in America.'

The old small town grapevine. Everyone knew everybody's business. 'Yeah, Philadelphia. Design and development for Roland.'

'Who's he?' Frank asked quickly, deadpan.

Ted laughed, shook his head. 'The keyboard company.'

'And now?' Frank bowed his head again, reached for an invoice, then resumed his typing.

'Oh, I just play to enjoy it. The odd club, tea dance, society; all sorts, really. What about you? You still play?'

'No.' Frank elongated the word. 'That all went when the kids came along. Gill's dad offered me a partnership in this.'

A silence settled. Frank tapped something into the computer.

Ted watched him for a while. 'You know, I'm sorry about the way I quit the band. The way I just left.'

'I wouldn't worry about it,' Frank said, glancing up, reaching for another invoice.

'But you did leave me standing there holding my organ,' Ted laughed, but Frank had started typing again.

'Shit,' Frank said and poked the delete button. He looked up at Ted. 'It was a long time ago. Another life. We've both moved on.'

'They were good days, though, weren't they? Furore.'

Frank smiled sadly. 'They're long gone, Ted. We're different people now.' Frank's gaze lingered on Ted for an instant, then he looked down and leafed through the stack of invoices. 'Sorry, Ted,' he said, 'but I've really got to get on…'

'Right,' Ted said quietly, the word hardly audible. For a few seconds he studied the top of Frank's head, the milky scalp under the steeled hair. 'Right,' he repeated. 'Well, I'd better be making off. It was good to see you, Frank.'

Frank didn't look up. 'Yeah, bye Ted. Nice to see you,' he murmured absently.

Ted walked slowly back along the aisle and out of the shop. As he crossed the car park, he pressed the button on his key fob. The lights on his car flashed. Hinging open the door, he glanced back at the building. He could feel a heaviness weighing on him, a sadness swelling inside. He sniffed then rubbed the side of his nose with a finger. The cool wind blew across him. He stared back at Frank's shop briefly, then he climbed into his car, swung the door shut and switched on the satnav. After a moment he programmed a new route. He was heading north, for one night in Nuneaton. They were always a good crowd in Nuneaton. And then it would be back home to the bungalow in Clacton for two days before he was on the road again.

Briefly, Ted hung his head, then he reached forward and twisted the key in the ignition.

TOM

It had been a strange few months.

Tom sucked the porridge from his spoon, turned and cranked on the hot tap. He swilled the dish and the spoon then left them to dry on the draining board. Dragging his hands under his armpits he glanced around the kitchen. There was food on the table, yesterday's leftovers: a half-eaten apple, turning brown now; lustreless chestnuts in a dish; on a place mat, a torn flatbread of some kind. Compared with the last house-share, this was benign. Here, there was no alcoholic shelf-stacker shouting on his phone, no fierce sex noises from the fireman and his girlfriend upstairs, and no Dado. Dado had been the silver-haired Slovenian who sat at the kitchen table all day, rolling cigarettes, playing on his computer, waiting for his girlfriend to return from work.

One night, Tom had been preparing a Bolognese. The meat was browning in the pan when Dado began to sharpen his knives. He'd just sat there, patiently honing a blade, his deep-set, slatey eyes fixed on Tom.

'So you think my girlfriend is attractive?' Dado had asked, sneering. That's when Tom knew he needed to move.

Tom pulled his mobile from his track-suit bottoms. Seven-fifty. He had to get to work. He'd picked up a couple of jobs, this one eight 'til eleven cleaning at a pub every morning, the other five 'til ten at night, Monday to Friday, waiting tables at The Swan. It wasn't much, but it was something. And he'd applied for a bar job at the golf club; was still waiting to hear back from them.

He jogged along the hallway, sprinted softly up the stairs and pushed into his room. He edged round the single bed and stepped over the pile of washing on the floor. As he pulled open the cupboard he glimpsed his reflection in the mirror, the blond, unruly hair, the patchy beard. He'd inherited the blond hair from his dad, his mum told him. That's all she'd ever said about him, other than that he'd left them; left before her parents had disowned her, before Tom was born. He reached into the cupboard, hauled out his blue fleece and pulled it on.

He ran back down the stairs and into the kitchen but slowed when he saw that Lucy, Cheng's wife, had appeared. She was wearing blue pyjamas, a pink, fluffy dressing gown and matching slippers; was holding a heavy curve-bladed cleaver. On the table in front of her, an onion rocked on a chopping board.

'See you later, Lucy.'

'See you,' she said, blinking, rubbing her nose with the back of her hand.

He pulled the back door closed behind him, crunched across the damp gravel. The March sky hung heavy, but there was a spring smell in the air, a rich, sweet freshness. Turning onto the main road, he strode quickly, watching the cars whip past, peering in at the drivers: a woman checking her eyebrows in the rear view mirror of her 4x4; a tanned man in a BMW, stroking his designer stubble. That's what he wanted, a life like theirs. A good life.

As he walked, he thought about Eric, his mum's new boyfriend. Tom had never liked the way Eric treated her, not from the moment he moved in last May. Tom had come home one day after an exam, and found her crying, heartbroken on the sofa.

'You don't have to accept this, Mum,' he'd reasoned.

'But I love him,' she'd said, like that was an excuse.

For months he'd been thinking about it, over and over, round and round, trying to make sense of it. He passed the primary school with its wrought iron railings, passed the flea-pit cinema, the tattoo place that was once a second-hand bookshop. His mum used to take him there when he was young. It had all changed in August. Tom had procrastinated, unsure if university was for him, and then he'd missed Clearing. That's when Eric really started.

'Time for you to move on, little manny,' Eric had said as they sat watching television one night. Tom could still see Eric's hard eyes glaring across at him, that tight curl of a half-smile. And his mum had turned away, pretending not to notice. It had all been inevitable after that. A couple of months later, he packed a bag and left when they were at work. He'd slept on a friend's sofa for a while.

Tom crossed the mini-roundabout, ran round to the rear of the pub on the corner opposite the kebab-house. He hammered hard on the locked door then turned, waiting. The old church's tower rose squarely over the red-tiled roofs, the gold hands against the blue clock face telling eight. There had been some Civil War skirmish in that church, musket balls buried in the wall behind the altar; no sanctuary given.

The bolts slid back with a snap, keys jangled, the lock graunched and the door groaned open. Gary, the landlord, held the door as Tom entered. He was fiftyish, stocky, and scowling.

'Morning, Gary,' Tom said, but Gary just bent and bolted the door.

Tom walked along the windowless corridor, past the toilets and into the bar. He unzipped his fleece, draped it over a barstool. Gary steered silently round Tom, then moved behind the bar, pushed through the door and clomped heavily up the stairs into the flat above.

After wiping down the bar and the tables, Tom retrieved the Henry vacuum from the cleaning closet. Occasionally, unconsciously, as he worked through the bar area, he touched the metal tube of the vacuum against a chair leg or a table, discharging the static build-up. His mind drifted.

When he'd saved enough money, he rented his first room in a shared house. There had been a junkie in the room downstairs, a girl. She was in the kitchen one day, slumped over the metal sink, peeling potatoes, but she turned when Tom entered.

'I'm Kate,' she said, squatting onto her haunches, cradling her knees.

'Tom,' he replied, looking at her matted hair, her grey skin, the track marks on one of her arms.

'I've written some songs,' she said, gazing down at the floor tiles. She was the first addict he'd seen up close. A couple of weeks later, she'd had a huge fight with her boyfriend; windows were smashed, the police called. He'd moved on soon after.

He bent and turned off the vacuum. As the motor quietened, he heard Gary and his wife arguing upstairs. They always argued. After replacing the vacuum in the cupboard, he picked a bottle of bleach from the shelf then wandered through to the gents' toilets. It was cold in there, had that urea smell. He elbowed open a cubicle door, squirted bleach into the bowl then reached for the toilet brush in the corner. This wasn't the gap year he'd envisaged. But it had pushed him to apply to university. There had been no real alternatives. So, now he had to wait, had to put up with things for a while…

*

He filled the mop bucket at the sink in the kitchen, splashed in some disinfectant. After he'd mopped behind the bar, he returned to the toilets. He'd discovered that he enjoyed mopping. There was something about the process he liked, the long, frictionless sweeps, the area methodically cleaned. He slopped the wet mop over the toilets' tiles, watching the steam rise from the cold floor, wrung out the excess water and wiped the surface again.

When he'd finished and put everything away, he found Gary in the bar, pouring money out of small bags into the till, the coins clattering into the plastic tray.

'That's everything, I think, Gary.'

The landlord didn't answer, didn't look up, he simply tipped another bag of coins into the till. Tom waited for a moment. Was he becoming invisible? He lifted his fleece from the stool and pushed in his arms. 'See you tomorrow.'

Outside, a watery sun lanced beams through the fracturing cloud. As he crossed the mini-roundabout, he saw the postman pedalling by on his bike, heading back toward town. The postman. Tom's strides lengthened, his pace quickened.

Cheng was in the kitchen when Tom returned. He was short and bald; was wearing a jumper with a wolf's face on it, and grey tracksuit bottoms, with blue, knee-length shorts over the top. He was a doctor of economics, but worked in a Chinese takeaway, taking orders, waiting to land a lecturing job.

Lucy was leaning her shoulder against the wall, peeling prawns. There was a tall mound of them in the large plastic bowl on the worktop beside her. Cheng barked something in Mandarin, continuing a conversation; Lucy was smiling, her head bowed.

'Morning, Cheng. Hello, Lucy.'

Cheng and Lucy spoke again. It sounded like they were squabbling, but Lucy laughed, a high-pitched giggle. Tom edged through the kitchen, unsure if they were going to acknowledge him.

'Lucy could have been a model if she didn't eat so many prawns,' Cheng said, his thick accent mutilative. 'Couldn't she, Tom?'

Tom laughed cautiously, unsure if it was a joke or if he was being drawn into a marital dispute. He sidestepped towards the door into the hallway. Lucy said something in Mandarin.

'Oh, what would I do without my Lucy to feed me?' Cheng asked.

'I'm not sure.' Tom inched nearer the door.

'Food is my life. So Lucy is my life.' Cheng pushed his face into a smile. 'How are you, Tom? Any letter?'

'Sorry, Cheng, I'm just going to check.' Tom pulled the door open and ducked from the room. As he walked along the hall, he heard Cheng revert to Mandarin.

The mail was scattered across the mat behind the door, lying in a pool of grey light. He stooped to collect it, fingered through the junk; among it were two letters addressed to him. There was movement at the top of the stairs. He turned. It was Wang, his other housemate, a young Chinese woman, twenty-two perhaps. Her hair was still damp after a shower; her sandals clapped against the soles of her feet as she descended.

'Hi,' she said, smiling, raising a hand as she reached the base of the stairs.

'Morning,' Tom said, blushing, smiling awkwardly.

He watched her push into the kitchen, then he heard Cheng's voice and a three-way conversation begin.

He dropped the irrelevant mail onto the low table, jogged up the stairs. In his room, he hesitated for a moment. He drew a breath, his shoulders rising, then exhaled loudly. Somehow, he already knew the replies would be rejections. He ripped open an envelope, withdrew the letter. As he read, a smile broke across his face. He opened the next, read again, his smile broadening, etching fine creases in his cheeks.

He thought of his mum. He should tell her. But she didn't care. He folded the letters, dropped them onto the bed. She was more interested in Eric. Being humiliated by Eric; being manipulated. Being in love. Tom stared out of the window, at the patches of blue sky. He supposed that was the lesson he'd learned: he was alone; had to look out for himself. He stooped to gather the heap of accumulated washing from the floor: a pair of jeans, tracksuit bottoms, socks, boxers. Standing straight, he glanced down at the letters again, then turned, collected the washing powder and fabric softener from beside the pile of books on the table.

He carried the washing downstairs, elbowed open the kitchen door and entered. Lucy was peeling another prawn while Cheng yapped over Wang's protestations. Cheng seemed to be repeating himself, but Tom couldn't be sure. Wang fell silent then Cheng tutted dismissively, shook his head.

'Women only think of shopping.' Cheng pursed his lips and shrugged at Tom.

'Oh,' Tom said, unsure what Cheng meant, uncertain how to respond. He leaned down and peered through the door of the washing machine, checking if it was empty.

When he straightened, Cheng was standing beside him. He was bowing slightly, looking up into Tom's face, his hands clasped sagely behind his back.

'You have a letter?'

Tom nodded, smiled knowingly.

'You have news?' Cheng held up both hands in anticipation.

'Good news.'

'This is good.' Cheng's smile cracked wide, revealing his chipped front tooth. He stepped forward and patted Tom on the arm.

'Accepted. Exeter and York.'

'Good,' Cheng said. 'Wonnerful,' he said more loudly. 'I tell them.' He turned and spoke to Lucy and Wang.

'Well done,' Lucy said carefully, looking up from the prawn in hand.

Wang smiled, beautifully, Tom thought, luminously.

As Cheng turned back to Tom, he widened his eyes, clicked his fingers. 'I have some point.' He shook a finger thoughtfully. 'We must celebrate. We have a meal. I invite you. Tonight.'

Tom squinted apologetically. 'Sorry, I can't tonight. I've got to work.'

'Saturday.' Cheng clicked his fingers noiselessly.

Tom smiled, nodded. 'Saturday.'

'Yes. My Lucy will cook. First class. Is that how you say?'

'First class, yes.'

'First class.'

'Excellent. Thanks, Cheng. Saturday it is.'

'Excellent. Saturday it is.'

Tom smiled at the way Cheng repeated his words. Cheng spun towards Lucy, began talking at her. Lucy laughed as she picked another prawn from the pile.

'Sorry, Cheng,' Tom quietly interrupted.

Cheng turned, grinning.

'Would you mind if I put some washing on?' Tom nodded toward the washing machine.

'Of course. This is your home.' Cheng rushed towards the washing machine, opened the door then stepped back and extended an arm towards it. As Tom crammed the washing into the machine, Cheng turned and started speaking in Mandarin again. The women responded simultaneously, volubly. Tom tipped some powder into the drawer, some softener, selected a cycle and set the machine to work, then left Cheng to bicker with the women.

Slowly he climbed the stairs. 'This is your home,' that's what Cheng had said. Tom closed his bedroom door. He looked around his room, the mess; books and other litter cluttering the table, the unmade bed, the bin liner of rubbish in the corner. Over the last few months, he'd forgotten what it was to have a home. And now, among people he could scarcely understand, he was accepted. Was that home? The place where you are accepted?

He picked up the letters, trapped them under an arm, then flapped the knotted duvet straight. Sitting on the edge of his bed, he unfolded the replies and read them again. The offers were unconditional. Leaning to one side, he pulled his mobile from his pocket. He knew his mum would be pleased. Surely, she would want to know. He scrolled through the numbers on his contact list, dialled. The call ended before a connection was made. He dialled again. Once more the call terminated. He leaned forward, his elbows on his knees, and stared at the phone. It felt like there was a heavy weight pressing down on his shoulders, as if gravity had intensified. He dialled the landline, listened to the ascending tone, the voice, 'This number has not been recognised.' How could they cut him out? What had he actually done? Staring down at the carpet, he slowly turned the phone in his hand, weighed it then tapped it against his chin. No, he refused to be excommunicated. He would go to see them. They'd be back from work at four.

★

The sun broke out as Tom draped the damp washing over the radiator. The light through the window cast shifting shadows on the wall as he hung his jeans and T-shirts on hangers from the curtain rail. He pulled his mobile from his pocket: 3.40. Time to go.

The spring afternoon had grown warmer with the sun's arrival. There were uniformed school kids returning home, passing him on the pavement. Some talked in pairs, some laughed in boisterous groups, some were alone. It was hard to believe he'd been like them once. He turned right at the pub where he cleaned, walked past the church, St Lawrence's, with its crop of lichen-stained gravestones, passed The Eight Bells. A streak of cars slipped by. Tom struck up the long hill, passed the sixth-form college where he'd been a student, then strode by the shady municipal graveyard. He veered away onto Hawthorn Lane, the road that ran up through the estate.

Now he was so close to home he began to shiver, his jaw juddering, but he wasn't cold. He turned onto the road where he'd grown up, a short cul-de-sac of small, eighties-built semi-detached houses. Eric's car was parked on the concrete driveway that sloped down to the house. Tom paused and glanced toward the end of the road; there were sheep grazing in the field. He could turn back. But why should he?

He walked along the driveway, pressed the doorbell, listened to the chime inside. The door opened. It was Eric. He was forty, tall, lean, had close-cropped hair. He drew himself to his full height, shifted so he blocked the doorway.

'Hello, Eric.' Tom still hadn't caught his breath fully.

Eric folded his arms.

'Can I come in?'

'What do you want, Tom?'

'To see Mum.'

'Why?' Eric was glaring at him.

'I just want to talk to her.'

Eric snorted. 'I'm afraid your mum doesn't want to see you.'

Tom felt the air rush from him, as if he'd been kicked. 'What?'

'You hurt her, going off like that. You hurt both of us.'

Tom tried to process the words, tried to grasp their meaning. 'But...but you didn't give me a choice.' Frustration tightened his throat. He took a half-step forward, then stopped, breathed in sharply, trying to gather himself. 'Can I come in or what?'

Eric pushed back his shoulders, set himself. 'No, Tom, you made your bed.'

Tom stared at him, not quite understanding.

Slowly, Eric surveyed Tom from head to toe. 'Look at yourself. You're a mess.'

'I'll be getting changed before work.'

'Are you on drugs?'

'What?'

'It's a simple question, Tom. Are you taking drugs?' There

was a cold certainty in Eric's tone, as if he held indisputable evidence.

'Of course I'm not.'

Tom stepped forward again, was preparing to barge in, but stopped when he saw Eric's arms drop to his sides, his hands ball into fists.

'I want to see Mum.' Instantly, Tom knew how childish, how desperate he sounded.

'You're not coming in here. Not until you've sorted yourself out.'

'There's nothing wrong with me.' He stood on tiptoe, trying to look round Eric, but couldn't see past him. 'Mum?' he called. 'Are you there?'

Eric took a step forward. 'I don't want you upsetting your mum any more.' He leaned forward, whispered, 'Not in her condition.'

Tom's stomach dropped. 'What's wrong with her?' he asked.

'She's pregnant.'

'Pregnant?' Tom stepped backwards, saw that cruel half-smile curl. 'Why didn't you tell me?' Without realising it, he was backing away. He paused on the pavement, looking down the driveway. 'Just tell Mum, I'm going to university. I've been accepted at Exeter and York.' He thought his voice sounded thin, distant. He stared at the upstairs windows, searching for movement, then, seeing none, he watched Eric close the door.

As Tom drifted down the hill towards town, his tears streamed, wetting the collar of his fleece. He dragged his sleeve over his face, but the tears continued to flow.

Saturday rolled round. When Tom returned from cleaning the pub, Cheng was sitting at the kitchen table watching the BBC news on his phone. He always said that it helped with his English. Lucy was preparing food, mixing something in a dish. Wang was helping. Tom passed through the kitchen, his head bowed, trying to avoid their attention. He hoped they'd forgotten about the meal.

He went quietly up to his room. Slowly, he prised off his trainers, pulled out his phone. Still no message from his mum. Why couldn't she have told him she was pregnant? He pulled off his fleece, dropped it on the floor, then lay down on his bed. For a while he listened to the cars passing outside. He closed his eyes, turned onto his side and curled into a ball.

When he next opened his eyes, the daylight was fading. Cooking smells had infiltrated his room. He checked his mobile phone. Seven o'clock. How had it got so late?

There was a gentle knocking at the door, so light that Tom wasn't sure it was a knock at all. He leaned up on his elbow, blear-eyed, listening. The double tap came again. Tom slowly swung himself to his feet. He stepped across to the door, opened it.

It was Cheng. 'You come?'

Tom looked at Cheng questioningly. He ran a hand through his hair, felt that tufts were standing out. He tried to smooth them with his palm.

'Your meal. I have invited two people. Friends.' Cheng held up two small fingers.

'Right?' Tom was trying to decipher what was expected of him. 'When?'

'Now.' Cheng moved across to the top of the stairs, went down a step, looked back and beckoned.

'I'll just be one minute.'

'One minute.' Cheng descended. Tom could hear the chatter downstairs, could hear the noise rise as Cheng entered the kitchen, then mute again as the door closed. Cheng's voice rose above the others.

Tom clicked on the light, squinted against the brightness. He stared into the mirror on the cupboard door, then licked his fingers and tried to lard down the tufts of stray blond hair. He didn't feel like celebrating. What was there to celebrate? Why were these people being kind? Was it pity? He could stay in his room, let them have the meal without him. They'd probably enjoy it more that way.

An unnerving silence fell when he entered the kitchen. He could feel himself blushing, embarrassed. The windows were fogged with steam, the air rich with cooking smells. A pan still boiled on the hob. Lucy stood near it, tapping at her phone. She turned when she heard the door close, smiled. There were people standing around the table, Cheng among them. He came crabbing across to Tom, with his bow-legged, bad-backed sidle.

'Come. Come in. Come and sit.' Cheng tapped Tom on the arm, bowled back across the kitchen and pulled out a chair at the head of the table. 'Come. Sit.'

Tom looked at the people. He saw Wang watching him, her face downturned. There was another Chinese man, twenty-two or twenty-three, Tom guessed, and a European woman of around thirty. She had a small bow in her hair. Cheng must have noticed Tom's uncertainty.

'Ah. Forgive me. You haven't met. This is Tian. And this is Jessika. They are friends from university.' Each extended a hand for Tom to shake.

'It's nice to meet you,' said Tom.

'Sit. Sit,' urged Cheng.

The table was loaded with food, dishes of sauces, a heaped bowl of noodles, a dish of grated cucumber, a dish of grated carrots. Tom, Cheng, Wang, Tian and Jessika sat. Lucy remained by the stove, tapping at her phone.

'Begin. Begin,' Cheng encouraged, passing Tom a bowl, 'Help yourself, Thomas. Have noodles.' Tom doled out some noodles into his dish with a fork. 'Have more,' Cheng urged, 'Lucy will bring more.'

'We are having noodles?' asked Jessika. From her accent, Tom guessed she was German.

'Ah, yes, noodles for long life. Noodles from the north. Rice in the south. Mainly. Now help yourself. You add your sauce and mix it.'

Tom looked at the sauces, uncertain.

'Now this is…' Cheng called something to Lucy in Mandarin. She replied without looking. He pointed to a light tan paste, 'This is sesame…' Then he pointed to a browny-black sauce, 'This is traditional turkey dish.'

'It is very traditional,' Tian said, speaking over folded hands, 'to mix in the cucumber and carrot.'

'This is the prawn,' said Cheng.

Tom spooned the turkey, carrot and cucumber onto his noodle mound, swirled it round.

Everybody else began helping themselves. Lucy brought over more noodles, tipped them into the dish, then resumed her vigil by the stove, ladling fresh noodles into the pan.

'You want chopsticks?' asked Cheng, suppressing a smile.

'I don't think I can,' Tom explained.

'Neither can I,' said Jessika. 'If you gave me chopsticks I would stay hungry.'

Everybody laughed. Cheng passed forks to Tom and Jessika. Jessika turned in her seat, looking back.

'Won't you join us, Lucy?'

'Later,' Lucy said, quietly.

'So, congratulations, Tom,' Cheng said, beaming his smile.

A chorus of 'Congratulations,' rose from around the table. Tom smiled, despite himself.

'So what will you study?' Jessika asked.

'Psychology.'

'Ah,' said Cheng, admiringly.

Wang nodded, smiled shyly.

'It is a fascinating subject, the human mind,' Tian said.

'And what do you study?' asked Tom, looking from Tian to Jessika.

'Anthropology, and the intrusion of government bodies...'

Tom's eyes widened with wonder. He didn't understood what she'd just said, but it sounded impressive.

'I'm studying a master's in sociology,' Tian said.

'Really,' said Tom appreciatively.

'This is good,' said Cheng, joyously, spreading his arms to signify the gathering around the table.

Wang laughed as Tom inexpertly wound the noodles onto his fork. She laughed again when they slipped off the fork and back into the bowl.

'I think the architecture of Spain is fascinating,' said Jessika, turning to Tian, picking up an earlier conversation, Tom presumed.

The conversation ran on. They talked of China, of the English language, of many things; they talked of love. And Tom's opinion was always asked. Not that he had many opinions to offer.

After a while, Cheng mentioned music.

'Wang is a very good singer,' he added.

'Mm?' Wang tilted her head, shook it, blushing, embarrassed.

'Yes,' Cheng confirmed. 'No need to be shy. You should sing,' he said to her. Then he spoke to her in Mandarin.

She raised her smartphone from the table, stroked it with

her fingers. She stood, held up a hand, mumbled something. Cheng nodded to her, then she tapped the phone. Traditional Chinese music began to play. She sang, her voice high, thin and melodious.

Tom stared at the table, then looked up at Wang. He had never been in this situation before. Wang sang a wistful trill, and Cheng, beside Tom, murmured appreciatively. He was tracing the music with his hand, in sweeping, winding movements, charting the ebb and flow of the melody. Wang trilled again.

'Hmmm,' said Cheng, his eyes closed, nodding his head.

And Wang sang on. As Tom listened, he looked around the table. This was family. He gazed down at his folded hands, and knew, that this, like all things was transient. That's what he'd learned; everything changes.

Wang sang her final note and blushed again. She glanced at Tom. He smiled, broadly, his face creasing with pleasure, then he clapped.

'That was beautiful,' he said.

Jessika reached across and stroked Wang's arm. 'That was very beautiful.'

'Beautiful. Yes,' Cheng said.

Wang sat, bowed her head. She was smiling shyly. Tom couldn't stop staring at her.

'But what is beauty?' Cheng asked.

'Lucy? Won't you join us?' asked Jessika.

It was an ending. It was a beginning.

GEORGE

He'd been clearing the borders for ten days now, digging out the plants and shrubs, then working it over again, turning the soil.

George drove the fork into the ground, levered back the handle, his white hair flopping forward. He sank the fork once more and pulled the handle towards him, breaking the moist earth.

'Don't you think it's time we retired?' Elsie had said.

They'd been sitting at the kitchen table, their empty plates in front of them. She'd wanted to slow down for a couple of years, but he'd always resisted. She reached across and placed her hand on his, wrapping her fingers under his palm.

'What would we do?' he'd asked.

'All the things we should've done,' she'd said.

'Like what?'

'Go on holiday… Sort out the garden…'

After forty-four years running a second-hand bookshop together, they'd finally closed down and sold up. They'd sailed off on a six-week cruise round the Caribbean then gone on smaller holidays, coach tours to Europe, around Britain. They'd even joined the bowls club.

'We should start the garden,' Elsie would occasionally say, laughing.

He stooped stiffly, grasped a dislodged weed, shook the soil from its roots and tossed it onto the lawn. The cool April breeze blew. Further along the border a robin hopped across the broken clods then flitted away. There wasn't much left to do now, only this section down to the short run of paving slabs by the back fence. He dug his fork into the ground again. If he'd just gone with her…

'Is there anything else we need?' Elsie had asked, buttoning up her coat.

'I don't think so.' He was peeling potatoes at the sink, preparing a cottage pie. They usually went shopping together, but he'd had a cold, hadn't felt like it.

He'd bent to one side so she could kiss him on the cheek. 'Won't be long,' she said. And then she'd gone.

George leaned on the fork handle, panting, trying to catch his breath. The dark-eyed houses across the back fence watched him, impassive. He hung his head for a moment. He should have kissed her when she was leaving. He should have been there…

'You OK, Dad?'

He turned. Emma, his daughter, waved from the back doorway then sank into the kitchen again. Since the funeral four weeks ago, she'd called in every day – a flying visit during her lunch hour, usually. He stabbed the fork into the turf and walked up the lawn towards the house, stamping the mud from his soles.

Tottering slightly, he toed off his shoes and stepped silently into the kitchen, the lino icy through his socks.

Emma was standing by the worktop beyond the fridge-freezer. 'Making progress?' she asked, pulling a carton of milk from her bag, then a pack of minced beef.

George pushed his hips forward, stretching the raw ache in his back. 'Slowly,' he said, straightening carefully.

She pulled open the fridge door and deposited the goods. 'Did you sort out with the bank?' She swung the door shut, looked across at him.

As he slowly rolled his aching shoulders, he spied the bottle of Famous Grouse. It was on the worktop, by the cookbooks in the corner. He should've put that away; she'd only go on.

'I can come with you, if you want.' She shouldered her bag, turned. 'Just say if you do.' She stepped across to the middle of the room then stalled. 'And don't forget Saturday.'

His forehead creased. 'Saturday?'

'You said you'd come for lunch, remember?'

'Yes, I know,' he lied. He arched his back again, watched

her. She was chewing the inside of her lip.

'Look Dad, if I can do anything to…'

'I'm fine, Emma,' he said, turning toward the back door. He gazed out along the garden.

'You should get your hair cut,' she suggested.

He hadn't been to the barber's since Elsie died; couldn't face the inevitable conversation.

'You're starting to look disreputable.'

George chuckled and moved toward the door. He leaned a hand against the jamb and slid his feet into his shoes, the backs folding under his heels.

'And don't forget the bank,' she urged as he scuffed out onto the lawn.

Night was fast falling, the light had thickened. George gripped his aching shoulder and surveyed his progress. He'd done more than he'd expected. There were only the paving slabs by the fence to tackle now. He would replace them with a flower bed; finish the garden with a flourish. He ambled back toward the house. The lights were on in the neighbouring houses while his remained in sullen darkness. And he could use the paving slabs to make a little courtyard area by the back door.

He kicked off his shoes, walked through the dark kitchen and thumbed on the light switch. On the worktop, the whisky bottle had been moved, there was an envelope leaning against it. Squinting, he hobbled across. Emma must have been rootling before she left; couldn't help herself.

He opened the envelope, fingered the contents: his passport, Elsie's chequebook, her debit and credit cards, a folded piece of paper. He teased out the sheet of paper. Elsie's death certificate. He dropped the bundle onto the table. Grimacing slightly, he reached up, opened the cupboard door and took out a glass. He slid the glass onto the worktop, then gripped the whisky bottle and unscrewed its top.

★

At 8.40 the next morning George was already walking down into the town centre. Cars clipped by in a steady stream, though he barely noticed. He walked past the shop they used to own, a tattoo parlour now, but didn't glance across. He wanted to be there when the bank opened, and then get home again as quickly as possible. A tall man with a leather satchel strode past. A local writer; he'd given a reading in the shop once. George couldn't recall the name. He steered round a woman walking her little girl up the hill to school.

'Four little monkeys jumping on the bed...' the mother sang as she passed.

He could see the bank's sign protruding from the wall. Beyond it though, half-hidden by the bend in the road... Was that the white canvas side of a market stall? It must be market day. Slowing, he glanced at the bank's entrance. It wasn't even open yet; he'd arrived early. He looked along the road again.

Perhaps there would be something for the garden on one of the stalls.

George bowled toward the counter just inside the bank's entrance. A woman was sitting behind it, looking at a computer screen, typing. She raised a tired smile toward him.

'Sorry,' she said. 'How can I help?'

His face flushed. 'Could I see someone about removing a name from a bank account?' He garbled the words slightly, wasn't sure they'd come out right.

'Of course,' she said calmly.

He reached into his coat, pulled the envelope from the inside pocket. 'I've got everything here.'

The woman looked at the envelope then back at George. 'Right,' she said, 'I think someone should be free.' She lifted the telephone receiver, held it to her ear and dialled a number. 'If you'd just like to take a seat...' She pointed to a row of chairs across from the cashiers' desks. 'Hello Zoe,' she said, 'I've got a gentleman...'

He drifted across the bank. There was no one queuing for the cashiers' desks; behind the glass screens the women were talking, their mouths moved but their voices were muted. On the far wall a large TV screen soundlessly reported news of a Tory rebellion. Something about the Brexit deadline. He smoothed down his hair with a hand then sat.

He contemplated the grey carpet for a while, then he considered the pot plant by the pillar. Which reminded him...

He reached into the side pocket of his coat and pulled out a fistful of packets. There had been a stall on the market that sold seeds and bulbs. He would go there again. He examined the packets. Sweet pea, delphinium, cornflower, freesia, nicotiana. There should be a colour scheme in the...

'Hello.'

George looked up. A woman was standing in front of him; she was small, wore glasses, had short, black hair. He crammed the packets back into his pocket, pushed himself to his feet and forced a thin smile.

'I'm Zoe,' she said. Assistant manager, her name badge announced. 'Would you like to come through?' She moved toward the glass-walled office, held the door as George entered, then closed it behind him. There were two chairs on the customer side of the desk, a high-backed swivel chair on the other.

'Please,' she said, hustling past him, 'have a seat.' She smoothed the back of her skirt then sat. 'So,' she hitched her chair closer to the desk, 'how can I help?'

'I'd like to take my wife's name off the account.'

'Right.' The woman nodded thoughtfully. 'Do you mind if I ask...' she began.

'She died,' he said. The words felt hollow, tasted unreal.

'Oh, I'm so sorry.' Her shoulders slumped.

'I've got these.' He held out the envelope, handed it across the desk.

'Well,' she said, extracting the envelope's contents, 'we can do one of two things. We can either remove your wife's name from the account, or we can close the account and open a new one.'

George nodded.

'Normally we would recommend that you shut the old account and open a new one. But it's entirely up to you.'

He stared at her, uncertain.

'Should we open a new account for you?' she prompted, leaning forward.

He nodded again and she began to type.

'This won't take too long,' she said, glancing up. 'I'll have to take a couple of photocopies, then you'll just need to sign a form.' She smiled.

He watched her fingers flicker across the keyboard. She was wearing a wedding ring.

George pushed the front door shut and hung his head. He looked along the hallway at the light washing across the kitchen floor. How could it have erupted like that? He'd just started crying; in front of a complete stranger. It was humiliating. A car rumbled down the road, the vibration rattling the letterbox. He stepped into the sitting room, glanced out at the street. Sunlight flared in the upstairs windows of the houses opposite.

Shuffling further into the room, he scanned the tall bookshelves on either side of the fireplace, spotted the Austen on the right-hand side, second shelf down. *Pride and Prejudice,*

1908 Macmillan edition. Worth £350 now. Elsie had found it at a car-boot sale just before they retired. He glanced over at Elsie's armchair, the antimacassar on the headrest. If he'd listened to her, if he'd retired earlier... He turned suddenly, walked out into the hallway and through to the kitchen.

Resting his hands on the cool Formica worktop, he gazed out through the window, along the garden. The borders were finished now. There was just the row of paving slabs by the back fence to lift, six of them in all. He reached into his coat pocket, scooped out a handful of seed packets, dumped them onto the worktop, dug out the rest.

'All the things we should've done,' she'd said.

He unzipped his coat, peeled it off, threw it onto the table then walked across the kitchen. He unlocked the back door, pushed outside then, pausing, he inhaled the cool, earthy air. A pigeon took flight from a rooftop across the back, its wings clapping. He sauntered along the lawn, paused by the shed and assessed the paving slabs. Probably prise them up with a spade, he decided, and if they offered any resistance he'd just knock them loose with the hammer.

He opened the shed door and cautiously placed a foot inside; the floorboards had rotted long ago. He hauled the lawnmower out of the way, the coil of hosepipe. There it was. Bending forward, he gripped the lump hammer's wooden handle. As he straightened, he collected the spade from its corner, then he retreated and let the door shudder shut. He leaned on the spade for a moment, let the hammer hang against his leg. Where should he begin? Did it even matter? Did any of it really matter any more?

*

He swung the hammer ferociously, with two hands. Bastard! The slab shattered, cracks ripping out to the edges. He smashed the hammer-head down onto a broken fragment, concrete splinters flying, clattering into the fence. He should have been there; should've gone with her. He hefted the hammer again, slammed it down. Bastard!

'What are you doing, Dad?'

He stood suddenly, turned and staggered to one side. Emma was standing halfway along the garden, staring at him, her arms folded, her shoulders bunched.

'Is everything OK?' She moved forward then halted, eyeing him, her lips pressed together.

'Just doing some clearing,' he explained.

She hitched her bag strap up her shoulder, nodded doubtfully.

He dropped the hammer and walked to meet her. 'I was just…' He stood beside her, turned and looked at the wreckage. He'd smashed five of the six slabs. 'I went to the bank…' He stared down at the flattened, muddied grass in front of him, and exhaled loudly, blowing out his cheeks.

'Are you all right?' She was watching him, wary.

George shrugged, tried to catch his breath.

'Have you been drinking?'

'No. I…' He laughed then trailed into silence.

'Look at your hands,' she said.

When he looked down, his knuckles were bloodied. He must have skinned them against the slabs. 'It's nothing' he said, drawing his hands back.

They stood in silence for a while, side by side. The birds were singing, a pigeon cooed, a pair of remote blackbirds trilled their call and response.

Emma glanced up at him. 'What time should I pick you up tomorrow?'

'Tomorrow?' he asked faintly.

'Lunch, Dad. You remember?'

He drew his shirt sleeve across his face. Wasn't there a garden centre near Emma's house?

'I thought it might be good to have a catch-up. We never seem to get the chance…'

There should be roses in the garden.

She turned and faced the house, squinted up at him. 'Should we say eleven-ish?'

'Mmm…'

'Are you sure you're all right, Dad?' She nudged him gently with her shoulder. 'I can phone in and take the afternoon off if you like,' she said. 'They wouldn't mind.'

He looked down at her, offered a lopsided smile. 'No, it's fine. You get back to work.' He stared at the shattered slabs. 'I should get on.' Stepping forward again he bent for the hammer.

Emma said something but he didn't listen. When he looked back, she was walking towards the house.

★

They'd been driving in silence for a while, had already breached the Surrey border. George glanced across. Her lips were puckered into a pout. She was chewing the inside of her lip, the way she always did when she was thinking about something. Should he mention the garden centre?

'I'm worried about you, Dad.' She was gripping the wheel with both hands, her eyes fixed straight ahead.

He watched the rolling fields beyond the low, litter-riddled hedgerows. The thick grass had a deep, rich lushness.

'I thought you were having a breakdown yesterday. Smashing everything up like that.'

George chuckled softly.

She clicked on the indicator, drifted down a slip-road. 'And then there's your drinking.' She left the comment hanging.

They were broaching the leafy outreaches of Farnham now. She drove on for a couple more miles, skirting the town's fringes, occasionally passing large, set-back houses. She slowed, steered round a couple of horses. George looked up at the riders, two women, one of them raised a hand in thanks.

'It still doesn't feel real, does it?' she said, quietly, as though to herself.

He touched a raw knuckle with his thumb, squinted slightly. 'Gardening helps.'

'What is it with you and the garden?' She was shaking her head.

The lane to the garden centre slid by, then she flipped on the indicator and turned down a subsequent side road. A few minutes later, she flipped on the indicator again and swept into her driveway, the gravel grinding beneath the tyres. It was a large house, modern but made to look antique, with flint panels between the brickwork piers.

She parked up, cut the engine, then reached behind her, retrieved her bag and delved into it. 'The boys have gone to the rugby,' she said, extracting her house keys. 'So it's just you, me and Paul.' She opened the car door, stepped out. 'Are you coming?'

Standing on the driveway, George hitched up his trousers and looked back at the neat, sweeping borders, the beech tree by the front gate. They had a man who did, apparently.

'I thought we might talk,' Emma said as George rounded the front of the car. She glanced back at him then she slid the key into the lock.

The smell of roasting chicken filled the house. He followed her along the hallway, trailed her into the rear lounge. Sunlight flowed slowly in through the French windows, drenching the room, burnishing the old upright piano against the wall.

She dropped her bag beside an armchair. 'Do you want a cuppa?'

'Go on. Thanks, Emma.' As she retreated, George wandered across to the windows and gazed out across the expansive back garden.

'Hello, George,' Paul said.

George turned. He'd always liked Paul. Grey-haired, bespectacled, tall and lean, he was a lawyer at a London bank.

'How are you, Paul?'

'Keeping out of mischief, you know.'

George looked down the garden again, 'What are those?' he asked, pointing.

'What are what?' Paul slouched towards George, stood beside him.

'Those bushes. The ones just past the birdbath.'

'No idea.'

'Do you mind if I have a look?'

Paul pushed the door open, straddled out onto the patio. 'Feel free.' He extended an arm in invitation.

George led along the lawn.

'Emma said you'd been gardening,' Paul commented, walking behind him.

George halted, looked at Paul as he drew level. 'It seems to help.'

'I think Emma could do with something like that.' Paul strolled on ahead.

'She seems fine to me,' George said, distracted.

Paul pushed his hands into his pockets, stalled. 'It's like the air's gone out of her.' He stared at the birdbath for a moment, then recalled himself. 'So which bush were you talking about?'

George strode forward. 'This one.' He stepped onto the border, ruffled the top of the bush with his hand. 'Something like this would be perfect down by the shed.'

'Sorry, no idea.' Paul raised his shoulders, stuck out his lower lip.

George wondered if they would have something like this at the garden centre.

'What are you two plotting?'

The men turned. Emma was walking towards them.

'Just admiring the garden,' George explained.

'Your drinks are inside,' she said, wheeling back toward the house.

★

Emma placed the cups on the coffee table. 'I've left yours in the kitchen, Paul,' she said, widening her eyes at him.

'Right.' Paul nodded then filtered from the room.

'Anyway,' she said, as though continuing a conversation, 'I wanted to talk to you, Dad.' She perched on the edge of the armchair. 'Properly.'

George rounded the sofa and sat. He hunched forward, his elbows on his knees, his head bowed, waiting. Was this about his drinking again? How could he tell her it was the only way he could sleep without Elsie beside him; the only way he could occupy the bed alone at night.

'I've been worried about you. How you've been behaving.'

There were clanking sounds from the kitchen.

'You're drinking every night.'

He lowered his head, arched his eyebrows.

'And now there's this gardening obsession.'

'It's hardly…'

'It's like you're withdrawing. And yesterday you were smashing things up.'

George tried not to laugh. 'I wasn't harming anyone.' He touched his knuckles, the torn skin stinging.

She looked at him sternly. 'But I don't know what's next, Dad. I can't…'

'You don't have to worry about me.' Bending forward, he reached for his cup, took a sip of tea.

'You're not going to do anything stupid, are you?'

'Like what?' He shot her a look, saw her press her lips together. 'What?'

'I just want you to know that you don't have to be on your own in the house.'

He lowered his eyes.

'Look,' she said, 'it's OK if you want to come and stay with us for a while.'

'Why would I do that?'

'But if you wanted to, it'd be OK.'

He shook his head, screwed up his eyes.

'I just wanted you to know you had options.'

George drew in a long, slow breath, sighed. 'Thanks, Emma.

But…'

'Just let me say it, Dad,' she interrupted, holding up a hand.
George stared down at the carpet.

'You can come and live with us. Paul and the boys would
love you to stay. Or…' She reached down beside the chair,
lifted the bag onto her lap then reached in and extracted a
brochure, 'they're building those nice retirement flats at the
other end of town. They're warden-assisted.'

George shook his head. 'No,' he said, firmly.

'I picked it up this morning. It's just something to think
about.'

He stared across at her. 'I'm not going to move, Emma, so
you can stop there.'

'No, I know. But you might want to in the future. If you're
not coping.'

He felt the anger prickle up his neck. 'Not coping? My
wife's just died.'

'I know that, Dad. But you could just have a look. For
future reference.'

'I am not moving.'

'I'm not saying you have to right now, but…'

'It's my home.' He glared across at her.

'And it was my home as well.' Her voice had risen; her eyes
were lacquered with tears.

'I know it was,' he admitted, bowing his head again.

'Is everything all right, you two?' Paul was standing in the
doorway. He had a tea-towel draped over his shoulder.

George reached for his cup and gulped down the contents. 'It's fine,' he said. 'Emma was just letting me know that I have options.' He placed the cup back on the coaster.

'Always good to have options,' Paul confirmed.

'I only want what's best for you, Dad,' Emma said.

He nodded, smiling wryly, his eyes half-closed. 'I know you do.'

'Sorry, Em, but could you come and check these?' Paul intervened.

Emma turned, looked back, scowling. Paul jerked his head toward the kitchen.

'I'm never really sure with honey-glazed parsnips,' Paul explained over her head.

'No one ever is,' George quipped. 'One of the mysteries of the universe.'

'Right,' Emma sighed. She gripped the arms of the chair, stood. 'What's the problem then?'

When she'd left the room, George glanced at the brochure she'd dropped on the coffee table. He shook his head then stood, zipped up his coat and quietly sidled into the hallway.

'He seemed fine to me,' Paul was saying in the kitchen.

George moved stealthily to the front door and opened it slowly, trying to mitigate any creak. He stepped outside, closed the door behind him, and hurried up the driveway. It should only take fifteen minutes to reach the garden centre.

Two hours later, having caught the bus home, he was kneeling in his garden. A blackbird was singing; somewhere children were laughing. Halfway along the border, he was excavating a pit with a trowel, mounding the earth at its sides. Would that be deep enough? He laid down the trowel, lifted the rose bush into the depression. A bit deeper, perhaps. He removed the rose then gouged out another scoop, and another.

'What are you doing, Dad?' It was Emma. There was a fierce edge to her voice.

He looked back over his shoulder. She was marching along the garden towards him.

'Do you know how worried we've been?'

'I just popped to the garden centre,' he said to the silvered fence in front of him.

'Popped to the garden centre? I don't believe this.' She picked her phone out of her pocket, thumbed a connection then held it to her ear. 'We were about to call the police.'

'There's no need for that,' he laughed.

'No, he's here,' she said into her phone. 'I'm not angry, Paul… No, I've got to go.'

George leaned forward, dug out another trowelful.

'For God's sake, can you just stop?'

He paused, his knees on the damp grass, his hands buried in the soil.

'What's happening, Dad? Have I done something wrong?'

He sat back on his heels, stared at the hole.

'Please talk to me. I want to understand.'

Wiping his hands on his thighs, he glanced up at her.

She was shaking her head. 'Is this the start of Alzheimer's or something?'

George laughed.

'Why are you laughing?' she demanded, her voice rising.

'No, Emma,' he said, quietly, 'it's not Alzheimer's.'

'But you just disappeared.'

He turned his face up towards her, smiling apologetically, one eye closed to the sun.

'Was it because I was talking about retirement flats?'

'No,' he said slowly.

'I wasn't saying that you should move into one. I was just saying it was an option, if you didn't want to be here, on your own.'

He dabbed at his face with his sleeve.

Emma stepped closer. 'You know I only want what's best for you, don't you?'

George smiled and raised his arm, holding out a soil-crumbed hand. She gazed at his dirty hand for a moment, then, reluctantly, grasped it.

'I just worry,' she said. 'What would I do if anything happened?'

Tightening his grip, he pulled her towards him, then downwards.

She crouched. 'You know you can talk to me, don't you?'

'Just come down here.' He shuffled to one side, making space for her, patted the ground.

She knelt beside him. 'This is going to ruin my trousers.'

'Why don't you put that rose in there?' He nodded at the plant.

She searched his face for an explanation.

'Watch those thorns,' he said, 'they're vicious.' He smiled. 'Go on. Just put it in there.'

She tugged up the sleeves of her sweater then bent forward, cautiously lifted the rose and positioned it in the hole.

'Right then,' he said, resting an elbow on the ground. He teased out the roots, until they extended in different directions. 'Let's fill it back up.'

They pushed the piled soil into the hole.

'I'm really not dressed for this,' Emma said.

'And press it down… Not too hard,' he coached. 'Does that look straight to you?'

She leaned back, tilting her head to one side then the other. 'I think so.'

He untucked a leg, placed a hand on a knee, stood stiffly. 'And now we just do this.' He circled the plant, compacting the soil with his heel. 'Grab the trowel, will you?'

As she picked it up, he stepped onto the grass and extended a hand again. She looked up at him, frowning, then reached out.

'Up you get.' He hauled her to her feet.

'Dad,' she said, standing, 'we really should talk about this. About what's going to happen.'

He led her across the lawn to where another rosebush lay unplanted on the opposite border. 'I thought we could put this one here.'

Gradually, he knelt again. 'You should dig this one.'

She was staring down at him. 'Why are you doing this, Dad?'

'Go on.' He nodded at the border. 'Make sure it's deep enough.'

'Right,' she said, crouching, kneeling, 'fine.' Bending forward, she began to trowel out the damp earth. 'I don't see why I've got to do it.'

'Just imagine what it'll be like this time next year,' he chuckled. 'All that colour. The scent.' He watched his daughter work, her hair swaying in front of her face. He settled back on his heels. 'Your mum would love them.'

It was a quiver at first, a sniff, then, Emma's shoulders were shaking. He watched her dig as it built, her back heaved. She covered her face with an arm, the trowel still in her hand.

George reached across and gently rubbed between her shoulders. 'That's it,' he said. 'You just keep digging.'

TONY & LYDIA

He didn't know why he'd agreed to move in with Lydia. It wasn't so much that he'd said yes when she proposed it; more that he hadn't quite said no.

Tony sat on the upper deck of the bus, watching the sun-gilded fields roll off to the horizon. Warm, wheat-smelling air ruffled in through the open windows, chatter swept forward from the college kids on the back seats.

He would have to tell her. He'd been putting it off for almost a month now, waiting for the right time. But he was supposed to be moving in next week. He thought of the previous evening. He'd been at her place. Lydia had been in her rocking chair, her feet on a footstool; he'd been slouching on the sofa. They'd been watching the ten o'clock news. The Prime Minister had announced her departure yesterday, her premiership broken by Brexit.

'It's up to us to heal the divisions,' Lydia had said.

'Who? You and me?'

'I just think that, as an artist, it's my responsibility to make a statement, to do something.'

'Really,' he'd said, drily.

She'd glared across at him. 'And what have you ever done, Tony?'

The bus leaned left at the roundabout, slowed, ground forward, nosing cautiously round the tight corner by the cricket pitch.

What had he ever done? The question had irritated him all day. He'd still been thinking about it during his final meeting with one of his PhD students.

'…explore the validity of the second person narrative position…' the student had been saying, something like that anyway; Tony hadn't really been listening. He'd been staring at the bookshelves along the wall of his office, contemplating the brief run of his own publications, two novels and a short story collection. Sometimes, when he was with Lydia, it was hard to believe he'd ever written anything.

The bus shuddered past the ugly modern housing estate, slowed to let off an old couple at the community hospital, tree branches slapping and scratching along the side windows. No, he was going to tell Lydia. The bus juddered into motion again. He'd been putting it off for far too long. Tony reached across and rang the bell, then sat, waiting, as the bus dawdled in the sclerotic snarl of traffic at the old railway bridge.

The bus drove away. Tony strayed from the pavement, set off across the green. It had once been used for the townsfolk's archery practice; now it was a space where kids kicked footballs, where people walked their dogs. Beneath the placid sky he strolled towards the run of bay-fronted Victorian semis across the far side. The heat had built through the day, had become a physical presence. Stepping from the grass, he crossed the dead-end access road, walked up the bricked path to Lydia's door, rang the bell. He swept sweat from his forehead with his fingers, flicked the drops over the wall into next door's garden, then watched Lydia's blurred advance through the frosted glass.

'Hello, Tony,' she said, smiling girlishly, bending slightly at the knee. Lydia was fifty-one but didn't look it. She was small, dark-haired and attractive; had a sparkle in her eyes. He followed her along the hallway. 'I was just telling Louis that my heart belongs in Istanbul,' she said, striding into the kitchen.

He pulled a face at the parquet floor. She often talked about the travelling she'd done in her twenties, the connection she'd formed with the Grand Bazaar. It was either that or something to do with her parents.

'Hello, Louis,' Tony said, pursing a tight smile as he walked into the kitchen.

'Tony,' Louis said, tossing his head. Louis was Lydia's new lodger. Twenty-three, tall and blond, he was wearing a T-shirt, shorts and trainers, was in preparation for a marathon.

'Louis went to Istanbul last year,' Lydia said, as though it was significant.

Tony leaned back against the worktop, folded his arms. 'How lovely.'

'Done much travelling, Tony?' Louis asked. He bent, gripped the backs of his ankles, stretching his hamstrings. He was training to be a social worker, had a self-assurance that set Tony's teeth on edge.

'Bits,' Tony said.

'But you've never been to Turkey, have you?' Lydia confirmed, throwing Tony a glance.

Louis performed a low lunge, his hands piled on a knee.

'No.' Tony shook his head slowly. 'So how far are you venturing today, Louis?'

'Twelve miles.' Louis pulled a foot up towards his buttock.

Lydia watched her lodger intently. 'Louis' mother was a runner.'

'Commonwealth Games,' Louis said, bouncing on his toes.

Tony cocked an eyebrow, sucked his teeth.

'You must have inherited the genes,' Lydia continued. 'It's a shame I can't say the same.'

Tony gazed out through the kitchen window, at the copse beyond the garden.

'I've always been such an ugly duckling.'

'You're not serious,' Louis said, becoming still.

Lydia giggled, shyly dipped her chin. 'No, really,' she said, 'my mother was very beautiful. I was on the tube with her when I was six…'

If Louis would just go, he could talk to her, tell her.

'…and one by one everyone turned and stared at her. People used to say that she didn't look like Elizabeth Taylor, but that Elizabeth Taylor looked like her.'

'She must have been amazing,' Louis said.

'Oh, she was a complete diva,' Lydia laughed, regally wafting a hand. 'Cruel, too…'

'So,' Tony rubbed his hands together, 'you look like you're about ready for that run, Louis.'

'No, you mustn't let me hold you up,' Lydia granted.

'I'd better go.' Louis paced across the kitchen, was out into the hallway.

'Lydia,' Tony rocked himself erect, 'there's something…' The front door slammed.

'I must just check the kiln,' she said, walking past him and out of the kitchen. Her footfalls receded along the hallway, faded into the lounge.

He heard the patio door drag open, took a step towards the sink, peered out of the window. She picked along the stepping stones across the lawn then jounced down the short stack of steps beneath the rose-tangled archway and walked across the garden's lower tier. She pulled open the door of the shed that functioned as her studio. He watched her plunge into the dark interior, then he turned and walked through to the lounge.

The lounge ran uninterrupted from the front to the back of the house. It was a shrine to Lydia's artistic endeavours. On top of the gas-fuelled faux log burner, in pride of place, was one of her 'architectural pieces', a dirty-green lozenge-shaped hunk of glass. A crack ran out from its centre, widened to a vast gap at the edge.

'Form over function, Tony,' she'd calmly explained when he'd asked whether the crack had been intentional. 'The kiln does its work,' she'd added gnomically. Lydia had come to art later in life. After nineteen years as a psychotherapist, she'd completed a Fine Art MA and let out a room to help pay the mortgage while she built her new career.

There were more pieces on the windowsill behind the sofa, on the hi-fi cabinet in the corner, on and under the coffee table. 'I couldn't possibly part with them,' she'd said, 'they mean far too much to me.' He considered the small lump at the end of the mantelpiece, a squat block, five inches tall, with green wavy lines ascending through it. He recalled how she'd told him she was going to call it *Ferns Interned*. He'd burst out laughing. 'Sometimes, Tony,' she'd said, 'you're very working-class.'

He rolled his shoulders, jerked his chin to one side, trying to shake the irritation. 'Very working-class.' She'd said that two months ago, just after they got together. He should have known then, that they were very different. But it had been good for a while. And he'd been grateful she took an interest in him. He'd been single for two years, after his previous girlfriend, Ellie, had left.

Tony walked towards the patio-doors. There were plants on the garden table outside, fuchsias, lilies, others he didn't recognise, all awaiting accommodation. He heard the soft click of claws on the floor behind him. Eddie, the old ginger cat, brushed past his legs, hesitated, looked up at him. It flicked its tail, then strayed outside and sat in the slatted shade under the table, contemplating a blackbird that mechanically pecked at the turf.

Lydia had re-emerged into full sun, was thoughtfully fondling the foliage of a camellia. She straightened, planted her hands on her hips and angled her attention at the unkempt privet straggling by the fence. Tony stepped outside. The warm June sun had drawn sweetness into the air.

'It's still cooling down,' she called. 'Should be ready tomorrow.'

He walked across the sun-seared lawn.

'I think you're going to like it though, the new piece.' She was assessing the privet again as he descended the steps.

'Lydia…' he began.

She turned towards him, shading her eyes with a hand. 'You don't want to trim the hedge, do you?'

'Not really.' He felt the need for an excuse. 'I'm a bit busy at the moment.'

'Doing what?' Amusement curled at the corners of her

mouth.

'I'm working on something.'

'One of your little stories?'

Tony inhaled sharply. 'Look, Lydia, I think we need to talk.'

'I really can't, Tony. Look at this place. It's Open Gardens on Saturday.'

'Tonight then?'

'I'm seeing Susan tonight. I think she wants to talk. And she's making an Ottolenghi.'

'It's good of you to find the time for Susan. And for Louis.'

She chuckled. 'You're not jealous, are you, Tony?'

Tony sensed the turn. He'd be fending off questions about his relationship with his parents in a minute; or she'd wheel out her transactional analysis.

'Maybe we could talk tomorrow. After work?'

She shrugged. 'Over dinner? I could cook.'

'Erm, if you like.'

Eddie padded across the grass towards Lydia. He paused in front of her, blinking in the sunlight, and mewed appealingly. Lydia leaned down, scooped up the cat and cradled him in the crook of her arm, rocking him like a new-born infant.

'How's my Edward Tedward?' she said. With his fluffy white belly exposed, his front paws hanging limp, Eddie was staring at Tony in a way Tony didn't particularly like.

'What did you want to talk about?'

'It doesn't matter.'

'We can talk now if you want to help me with the garden?'

'No, it's fine.' Tony turned, planted a foot on the lowest step. 'It'll wait.' As he climbed to the garden's upper tier, he raised a hand in farewell.

'Now then, Eddie Teddie, where should we put those fuchsias?'

Tony strode up the long hill to town, the traffic whipping by, incessant. A flash of colour in a garden caught his eye. A red Labour sign on a post had toppled behind the low wall. How had he not told Lydia? Somehow, it was never the right time. It was a skill she had. He passed the church, the Conservative Club, the newly built retirement flats on the corner of Queen's Road. There were men talking outside the pub across from Marks & Spencer, the typical type: shorts, flip-flops, tattoos. He strode by the dry cleaner's, the Turkish barber's, passed the earth-smelling greengrocer's then crossed the side street beside the Boots store.

The girls in the street were wearing their summer clothes. He watched their bronzed shoulders and felt that feeling again, the leaden sense that he'd missed out on something. Since Lydia had decided he was moving in he'd felt it more and more. And he'd started looking back. He'd spent a few afternoons last week trawling Facebook, searching out people he used to know. Their lives all appeared so complete, so idyllic. He'd sent a few messages, tried to reconnect. But no one had replied, except the person who wrote back to say he was too busy to reply.

At the top end of town his eye was drawn by the war memorial, the domed mound of stones outside the Assembly Rooms. He paused at the mini-roundabout waiting for a gap in the traffic. He would definitely tell Lydia tomorrow. No more running away.

Tony let the front door clump shut, sniffed tentatively. There was only a faint smell. He would clean the kitchen in the morning.

The curtains in his bedroom were still drawn. He slung his satchel onto the unmade bed, toed off his shoes, unbuttoned his shirt, removed it, lobbed it towards the bed. It fell short, flopped damply onto the carpet. He wrenched his belt loose, let his chinos sag to his ankles, kicked them off. He scavenged among the discarded clothes on the floor, picked up his shorts, pulled them on, hopping sideways as he tried to insert his second leg. Not one of your little stories. That's what she'd said.

Books lined the shelves along the wall in the spare bedroom, his study. He sat at the desk beneath the window, lounging back, gazing at the blue sky above the roofs of the next street along. A distant plane glinted in the sun, laying a long vapour trail. From next door's garden came the grind of trampoline springs, the squawking laughter of children playing.

Tony contemplated the pad on the desk. No, this wasn't one of his 'little stories'. This was a thing of beauty. He'd begun work on it a week ago. *The Jazz Cats*. And why shouldn't he write a children's book? Every talentless F-grade celebrity was cashing in, why shouldn't he? But this was something different; a touch of class. He flipped back to the pad's first page, skimmed the scrawled outline.

A group of four suburban cats, who live on the same leafy street, have formed a criminal gang. They use false names. There's Miles Davis, a young gangling ginger who's slightly stupid; there's Dizzy, a tortoiseshell who wears a beret; the second-in-command is Charlie Parker, a pink-nosed black and white who wears shades and has missing teeth; their leader is a hugely fat, scruffy cat with a persistent cough they call Mingus.

It was perfect. He smiled, turned to the last page he'd written.

The cats sat in a circle looking down at it. It was hairy, didn't move.

'You did well,' Mingus said. He coughed, then slowly twisted his neck and scratched behind his ear with a slow flicking back paw.

'I just did what you told me, Mingus. It was easy,' Miles boasted. 'I bit into it and ran off without letting go.'

'I don't like it,' Charlie Parker said. He tongued his toothpick to the other corner of his mouth. 'We've never done anything like this before.'

'We're moving into the big league now,' Mingus said.

'What the bebop is it?' Dizzy asked. He prodded it with

his paw but it didn't respond.

'Yeah, what is it, Mingus?' Miles echoed. 'It doesn't wriggle like a mouse.'

'It's no mouse,' Mingus said. He reached into his matted fur, pulled out a small pair of scissors.

Charlie Parker saw the steel glint, stood, sat again. 'What you going to do with those, Mingus?'

Mingus ignored him. 'It's called a toupee, Miles.'

'I don't like it, Mingus,' Charlie growled.

'Hold it down, Dizzy.'

'Yeah, hold it down, Dizzy,' Miles parroted.

'Shut up, Miles,' Dizzy hissed, 'or I'll bebop you right in the salt peanuts.'

'Shut it you two,' Mingus wheezed.

'You can't do this,' Charlie Parker protested. 'I never agreed to a wignapping.'

'Ah, stop moanin' Charlie Parker. Just think what we can do with the ransom money.'

Granted, Tony thought, it might not actually be for children, but it was in that sort of area. And there was nothing else on the market like it. There must be some niche for ironic pseudo-children's literature with esoteric jazz references. And everyone liked cat stories. A bit of polish, slick it up. He could see a future in this. Sequels, prequels, a series.

Tony picked up his pencil, scribbled.

'You're going to get us sent to the cattery,' Charlie said.

'What's a cattery?' Miles asked.

Tony tapped the pencil against his chin, closed his eyes. If he wanted to make the stories truly representative of society, he would need to capture the social diversity of modern Britain. He could have cats like Ravi Shankar, Baaba Maal and Julio Iglesias living up the road. Could you call a cat Abu Tabby, or would you have to stick to musical references? He could work that out. But with this model he could address any social issue, and show how the cats live together in a multicultural society. No, this wasn't just a little story. This was something meaningful, significant even.

Tony walked slowly across the green. The sun beat down, a gentle breeze blew, the traffic droned. 'Lydia,' he rehearsed, 'I'm just not ready for this level of commitment.' Would that open him up to one of her lectures? 'Lydia, I've really enjoyed our time together…' No, she'd turn that round on him, like she always did.

He knocked at the door, stepped back. He was just going to come straight out with it. That was by far the best policy. She could react however she liked, she'd just have to deal with it. And he could fall back on the 'It's not you, it's me' tactic. That's what Ellie had said.

Louis pulled open the door then turned and sauntered back along the hallway. He wandered into the kitchen. Tony pushed the door closed behind him. The scent of frying onions hung in the air.

'Oh, really…absolutely…' She was upstairs, on the phone, he assumed.

He paused at the base of the stairs, listening.

'But…mmm…when I went to Jenny's, I just thought, her shrubs are so much better than mine…'

Tony walked through to the kitchen. Louis poked at the pan on the hob with a spatula.

'Smells good,' Tony said. Now that he'd stopped walking a sweat had begun to roll.

Louis ignored him. The cat clattered in through the cat flap, strolled across the kitchen and out into the hallway. Tony studied the back of Louis' head. Even that was smug.

'So, how's the course going?'

'Yeah, it's going.' Louis briefly looked back over his shoulder, then stirred the onions again.

Tony drifted out into the hallway, dabbed at his face with the cuff of his shirt. Lydia was still on the phone upstairs. 'But she's such a dear…'

If she would finish on the phone he could talk to her, tell her. He shook his head then walked through the lounge, towards the patio doors. The cat was sitting on the doormat. It stood as he approached, arched its back, mewed.

'Fuck off, Eddie,' Tony said quietly. Eddie stepped out onto the crazy paving, sat for a moment, then lay on his side, basking nonchalantly.

There was movement overhead, dull thunder on the stairs.

'That smells wonderful, Louis.' Lydia's voice bled through

from the kitchen. 'I was upstairs salivating.'

Tony pushed his hands into his pockets, watched a pink petal drift down from the rose-wound arch.

'Would you like some?'

'No, I'm supposed to be cooking for Tony.' Tony noted her rueful tone.

'He's lurking somewhere.'

Lydia tittered. He turned as she bustled into the lounge.

'Hello, Tony,' she twinkled. She walked towards him, raised a cheek for him to kiss. He bent, obliged. She brushed past him, sidestepped outside. 'How's my Eddie Teddie?' she said, stooping to scratch the cat between the ears.

Tony inhaled deeply, pushed back his shoulders. 'Lydia,' he said gravely. 'We need…'

'Come along, Tony.' She looked back at him, tilted her head towards the garden. She skipped down the steps, crossed to the shed, paused beside it and bent low. Tony slowly followed her, then stalled at the top of the steps when he saw her straighten, a paintbrush in her hand.

'I've already taken the lid off for you.'

'What?'

'The paint. It's all here for you.' She gestured towards the shed.

'No, I…' He held up his hands.

'Come on, Tony. Don't be a child.'

'I'm not being a child, Lydia.'

'You're behaving very badly.'

He felt his anger surge. 'How am I behaving badly?'

'You're shouting, Tony. In public.'

'I'm not,' he began loudly, then dropped to a savage whisper. 'I am not shouting.'

'You know how much Open Gardens means to me.'

'I don't give a shit about Open Gardens,' he said, his voice rising.

'But it'll be utterly humiliating…' She held the paintbrush out, moved towards him.

Tony dipped the brush in the paint, then daubed it on, smoothing it out with long, resentful strokes, from left to right, from right to left. And she'd just wandered off inside. As soon as he finished the shed, he was going to tell her.

'I've always thought Clive a seriously difficult man… I don't know how Susan puts up with him.' Her voice leaked out.

He turned. She was standing at the open bedroom window, talking on the phone. She waved at him, smiled.

He faced the shed again. What was he doing? This was how modern slavery worked. It was exploitation. He wasn't the handyman. He was an author with an international reputation. Well, he'd been translated into Norwegian. One of his books was at 80,000 on the Amazon rankings. He hung his head, the warm light beating against the back of his neck. It had gone on too long. No, he would just tell her, point blank. He was sure she would be fine about it.

He bent and dipped the brush into the paint.

'The pasta's on,' she said. She'd been inside for over an hour. 'You've done a very good job.' She jogged him amiably with her shoulder, admired the shed.

He shrugged, then bent and laid the brush across the paint pot's rim. She moved forward, opened the studio door, stepped in.

'Oh,' she gasped, 'come and look, Tony.'

Tony tutted then shuffled into the shed. It took a moment for his sight to adjust. On the right, there were jar-filled shelves above a long bench. The centre of the space was occupied by the large, electric kiln, its lid open. Lydia leaned in, shifted something. 'Just grab the other side will you?' she instructed.

They lifted her latest creation out of the fired-clay mould, carefully carried it into the daylight, Tony reversing towards the house. It was a large misshapen glass dish with a blob of blue in the centre. There were cut out copper-foil handprints layered in beneath the surface, forming a circle around the rim.

They lowered it onto the coffee table in the lounge. From out the front of the house came the yelps of teenagers kicking a football on the green.

'What do you think?' she asked, standing back, tilting her head to one side.

'Mmm…' Tony pressed his lips together. The hand prints were repetitions of the same single hand, a left hand that was flipped over alternately, so the thumb was met by little finger.

'What do *you* think?'

'I think it's rather successful.'

'Mmm…'

'The pasta,' she said, scurrying past him and through to the kitchen. Pans clanked.

Tony eyed the dish again, the clumsy blue blob at the base, the handprints.

'Can you set the table, Tony?' Lydia called through.

She was tipping the pasta into a colander when Tony wandered into the kitchen. Water rattled in the metal sink, a cloud of thin steam billowed, dispersing. She shook out the water. 'I was thinking of putting it in the exhibition,' she said, continuing a conversation. 'Did I tell you Emsworth have been in touch?'

'Who?' Tony pulled open the cutlery drawer.

'The gallery at Emsworth. I thought they would be.'

He didn't know Emsworth even existed.

'Don't forget the mats, Tony. There's a good clientele there. Emsworth. Lots of money. Yachting crew. She said she really likes what I do.'

Lydia kept talking as she spooned the penne onto the plates then crowned the pasta mounds with sauce. Tony positioned the forks on the tablecloth. He just needed to find the right moment, the right opening.

'And did I tell you I'm going on a march with Judith? It's so important to foster these contacts.' She carried the plates across to the table. 'She's such a lovely person. Always has something nice to say about everyone.' She placed the plates on the mats. 'She meditates.'

'What's the march about?'

'Brexit, I think. Or the environment. I'm not actually sure.'

Tony rolled his eyes, sat. He forked some pasta into his mouth.

'…you wouldn't believe how much work Susan had put into the Ottolenghi…' Lydia sat, hitched in her chair.

For a while Tony watched her mouth move, words were pouring out, but he'd stopped listening. His mind drifted to *The Jazz Cats*. Should Charlie Parker sabotage the wignapping? Was he the yang to Mingus' yin?

'…but Clive is a seriously peculiar man. There's something very odd about him…'

Tony quietly ate his meal while she soliloquised. When he'd finished he slid his fork onto the plate, sat back. He drew a deep breath, gripped the table's edge.

'…it'll never be a perfect garden but it can be pretty. And Miriam has offered to make cupcakes…'

'Lydia,' he said.

'…and she said Bruce was the only single man in town worth thinking about. But he's quite mad, a mathematician, brilliant but…'

'Lydia.'

She frowned at him, fine creases crinkling her forehead.

'I wanted to talk about moving in.'

'Have you started packing?'

'Well that's the thing. No, I haven't.'

She watched him, waiting.

'Look, I'm not sure I'm really ready to move in.'

'What do you mean?'

'I'm just not ready for that sort of commitment.'

'Don't be such a teenager, Tony.'

'I'm not being a teenager, Lydia.' Tony ran his fingers through his hair, then massaged his forehead. 'I've just got a lot on at the moment.'

'You've finished marking, haven't you?'

'Yes, but I'm writing something.'

'You could write it here.'

'I don't think I could.'

'Why not?'

'I just don't think it would work.'

Lydia sat back, her dark eyes glittering. 'What are you writing?'

'I don't want to talk about it.' He leaned forward, rested his elbows on the table.

'Well, I think you're going to have to if it's going to stop you moving in.'

'I don't want to jinx it.'

'Don't be ridiculous, Tony. Tell me.'

'It's called *The Jazz Cats*,' he said reticently.

She threw back her head, laughed throatily. '*Jazz Cats*?' Her eyes sparkled.

'This is why I didn't want to discuss it.' He rested his

forehead on the heel of his hand.

'What's it about?' She attempted to compose her features.

'It's sort of a children's book.'

'What do you know about children?'

'Enough.'

'Come on, Tony. A children's book?'

He slouched back in his chair. 'This can put me back on the map, Lydia.'

'Grow up. You're going to have to stop chasing your little dreams sometime.'

'I'm a published author.'

'Do you know how pompous you sound?'

'Look,' he said, 'I've got a lot of pressure riding on this...'

'Pressure? Everyone has pressure, Tony, and they just have to deal with it.'

Tony shrugged.

'I've got pressure. It's Open Gardens this weekend. And Emsworth's coming up.'

He shook his head. 'Look, Lydia, I really don't think this is going to work out.'

'What's not going to work out?'

'This.' He waved a hand, generally. 'Us.'

'That's it, isn't it?'

'What is?'

'I knew it.'

'Knew what?'

'This all goes back to your mother, doesn't it?'

'What?'

'No one's as good as your mother, are they?'

'What are you talking about, Lydia?'

'I think you know.' She nodded slowly, meaningfully.

'Know what? This is nonsense.'

'Before you have a grown-up relationship, Tony, this is the stuff you're going to have to deal with.'

'But I don't have a problem.'

'Have you had any counselling?'

'Why would I?'

'I think you should.'

'I don't need counselling. I don't have a problem.'

'Evidently you do.'

He inhaled slowly, deeply. 'Look Lydia, I'm sorry you feel this way...'

'Good. You should be sorry. You can't treat people like this, Tony. You're an adult. You can't always make excuses.'

'I wasn't making excuses.'

She laughed playfully, reached across, squeezed his hand. 'We talked about this, didn't we? Do you remember?' she said gently, as though to a child. 'We agreed. You'll let your house, move in here, and we'll be comfortable. I won't need a lodger then... We can have the place to ourselves.'

He was still shaking his head when she moved her hand onto his thigh.

'Let's not fight, Tony. I thought we were good together. We have fun, don't we?'

'I wouldn't call it fun, exactly.'

'You do still find me attractive, don't you?'

★

He was woken by a soft nuzzle against his ear, a moist touch against his forehead. For a moment he kept his eyes closed, recalling where he was. He could feel Lydia beside him. Again there was a gentle hairy jostle against his head.

He winked open an eye, saw the furry ginger mass near his face. He raised an arm, shoved the cat towards the headboard. 'Piss off, Eddie.'

Lydia groaned, reached up to comfort the cat. 'Is he being mean to you, Edward Tedward?' Eddie mewed his complaint.

'He was trying to rub his arse in my face,' Tony croaked.

'Don't be crude, Tony.' Eddie settled in the valley between them, mewed again. 'You just want feeding, don't you, Eddie Teddie?'

Even now, Tony thought, after they'd had sex, albeit muted sex so they didn't disturb Louis, he was second-best. To the cat. Tony threw back the duvet, swung his legs from the bed, sat on the edge of the mattress. How long had he been asleep? The light was withdrawing from the room. He stood, scouting out his boxer shorts among the gathering shadows. He found them under the window. As he stepped into them, he glanced out onto the garden. He'd actually done quite a good job with the shed. He reached down, picked up his rumpled chinos.

'What are you doing?' Lydia asked.

'I'm getting dressed.'

'Why?'

'I'm going home. I've got work to do.'

'Not your ridiculous little story. I thought you were joking.'

'Yes, my ridiculous little story,' he said, sighing as he pulled up his trousers.

Eddie mewed again.

'Yes, I know Eddie. Poor chap. I'll feed you in a minute.'

Tony buckled his belt.

'You do remember you promised to help me with Open Gardens.'

'I don't think I did.' He sleeved into his shirt, began to button it.

'Well, you didn't refuse.'

'You never asked me.'

She chuckled. 'I just assumed you would...'

Tony tugged down his shirt, flattened out the creases with the palm of his hand. He must have left his satchel downstairs.

'What day are you thinking of moving in next week?'

'Mmm...' he said, pushing his feet into his shoes. He would tie them later. He shouldn't have slept with her. It had muddied things.

He walked around the bed, leaned down and kissed her on the forehead, then walked across the room, his shoelaces rattling on the varnished floorboards. When he was in the doorway he turned back, looked at Lydia. Eddie was standing on her chest, pressing his nose to hers.

'Actually Lydia…' Tony remembered his trousers, reached down, zipped his fly.

'Mmm?'

'I'm not going to be moving in…'

She rolled onto her side, facing him, her eyebrows rising to high arches. Eddie mewed at his displacement.

'In fact, I think I'd like to take a break from…us.'

'Take a break from us?' She raised herself on an elbow. 'What are you talking about, Tony?'

'I'm saying it's over, Lydia. You and me.'

She smiled at him, frowning from under her mussed hair.

'I just don't think it's working out.'

'What about Open Gardens?'

'Sorry, Lydia.' And then he was gone, out onto the landing, stepping down the stairs two at a time.

'Tony?' Lydia called, but he didn't reply. 'Tony!'

He dodged quickly into the kitchen, to collect his bag. Louis was there, cupping a bowl of heaped cereal. Tony spied his bag hanging from the back of the chair.

'Louis,' Tony said sharply, lifting his bag, shouldering it.

'Aren't you the gentleman?' Louis smirked.

Tony slammed the door shut behind him. And he'd had enough of that obnoxious little turd. Lydia could keep him. They'd be happy together, talking about Istanbul or whatever.

Tony set off up the long hill to town. It was cooler now, the grey evening was falling, the traffic had thinned. Across the road a street lamp sputtered into life. He settled into a loping stride. At least it was done. He'd leave it for a few days before he rang to make sure she was OK. But he wouldn't change his mind this time. He wouldn't let her talk him round again. He had to concentrate on the things that mattered. Another street light flickered on. Now then, Charlie Parker, what are we going to do about this wignapping...?

HEATHER

She'd been working at the golf club for almost a month now, and she was still only part-time.

Heather snapped off the beer tap, lifted the glass onto the bar.

'I mean, I like Tom,' she said. 'He's all right.'

Victor gulped back his lager.

She studied her fingernails, thumbed a sharp jag of skin. 'I still can't see what Barbara's got against him.'

'She doesn't like anyone.' Victor pushed up the peak of his cap, massaged his leathery forehead. He was the greenkeeper; lived in the pre-fab bungalow beside the clubhouse. 'Single too long,' he reflected.

'I know she's a bit...' she turned down the corners of her mouth, '...you know...but I actually like it here.' She looked along the clubhouse; the dull daylight sheened on the laminated table tops in the dining area. 'It's better than the retirement home anyway.'

Victor drank again; the wine fridge shuddered. She gazed out through the slats of the Venetian blind. The trees lining the first fairway were swaying sedately in the soft May breeze.

A heavy thump swung Victor round. He peered past the kitchen towards the car park, then turned back suddenly, drained his glass and slid it onto the bar. 'Get rid of that, will you?' He tugged down his cap then strode across to the door and pushed it open. The door clumped shut as he hopped down from the patio to the path beside the putting green. She gathered the abandoned pint pot and dumped it by the sink, then collected the cloth and anti-bac spray from behind the taps. When she turned, Victor had already vanished.

She misted a stretch of bar; the building sucked a breath. Barbara was backing in from the foyer, a bulging plastic bag suspended from either hand. Sedulously, Heather worked at a tacky patch of congealed beer as Barbara bustled through the dining area then swerved towards the kitchen. The swing door squealed open, slapped back a couple of times. Heather cleaned along the bar, rounded its right angle, wiped the short run to the wall where the fruit machine flickered in its corner. The swing door squealed again.

Barbara paused by the bar, was jabbing at her smartphone, shaking her head. Heather glanced across. The ruddy cheeks, the thin top lip; Barbara was a woman forever on the verge of anger.

Barbara tutted, continued to tap at her phone. 'Victor been in?'

'Haven't seen him,' Heather said, leaning back against the shelves beneath the upturned spirit bottles.

'Bone idle…' Barbara swiped the touchscreen. 'Worse since his wife left.'

Apparently she'd taken the children and moved back to Ireland.

'I don't believe this. The committee wants a new menu.' Barbara sounded exasperated. 'How am I supposed to make people eat *here*? I'm not a miracle worker.'

Heather scanned the small blackboard hanging on the wall. Bacon rolls; ham, egg and chips; it was hardly haute cuisine.

Barbara pocketed her phone. 'Right, I've got to go. There's some stuff in the kitchen you'll need to put away.'

'You going out to play golf?' Heather asked. It's what Barbara usually did.

'Working from home,' Barbara said. 'This bloody menu thing.' She set off along the clubhouse. 'And let me know what time Tom gets here,' she called from by the door. 'I'm not having him take the piss as well.'

Heather held the mobile phone to her ear.

'I'm putting them back on now… Yeah, before my husband gets home.' She ran a finger along the windowsill, assessed the dust on her fingertip then rubbed it away with her thumb. Behind her the door from the foyer wheezed open; floorboards groaned.

'Of course I enjoyed it. Did you?' She looked out towards the row of old oaks that marked the course's boundary. 'Just use a damp cloth,' she advised. She turned, saw Tom slouch onto a barstool. 'OK, honey… Yep, you too. Bye, hun.' Lifting the phone from her ear, she tapped the screen to disconnect. It was easy money, but there was something very odd about the men who rang her.

'How's it going, Tom?' she called, walking towards the bar.

He grated a heel back across the coarse, ridged carpet. 'Can't stand this place.'

Heather paused in front of him, eyeing the network of creases in his shirt, the unbuttoned cuffs, the paltry fluff around his jawline. 'What's happened?'

'Got my final warning yesterday, didn't I?'

Heather shook her head, her mouth open. 'What for?'

'I've absolutely no idea.' He threw a hand up, let it drop. 'Says I'm consistently late.'

She frowned, checked the time on her phone: 2.55.

'I wouldn't mind if I'd actually done anything wrong.'

'You're not going to quit, are you?' She stepped through the open bar hatch, then into the small unlit room at the back where she collected her bag and denim jacket from the top of the long chest freezer.

'I've started looking,' he called, 'but there isn't much about…'

She dropped the bag onto the stool beside Tom, pushed her arm into the jacket sleeve.

'…just a couple of cleaning jobs.'

'I'd apply for them if I were you.' She delved into the other sleeve, tugged the jacket straight.

'Is she having a go at you?'

'She tries,' Heather said knowingly. 'Victor said she's like this with everyone.'

'I don't get it. What have I done?'

'I'm pretty sure it's not you. I mean, I don't think you've actually done anything wrong. But if I were you,' she said gently, 'I'd just move on and put this behind you.'

Tom slowly shook his head. 'I wish I'd never come here.'

She reached out, soothingly stroked his arm. 'Just hang in there, Tom. You'll find something. And you'll be going off to uni in a couple months.'

He smiled mournfully. 'Thanks, Heather.'

She felt herself blush. 'Right,' she said, zipping her bag shut, 'I've got to go.'

★

Heather twisted the key in the ignition, cut the engine. The red brick retirement home would once have housed an affluent Victorian family and its staff. She unfastened her seatbelt, let it retract. As she reached over to the passenger seat for her bag, she glimpsed the pile of washing on the back seat.

And that had to be ironed by morning if she wanted to be paid. She settled the bag on her lap, opened it, pulled out her phone. It was a shame for Tom, but what could she do? She tapped out the text.

'Sorry to disturb you Barbara. I know you must be busy. Tom only arrived at 3.20. Best wishes. Heather.'

She stared at the blank screen for a moment, then deleted 'Best wishes,' typed in 'Apologies,' and sent the message.

★

She carried the pile of folded tablecloths into the dining room of the retirement home. It was all so beige. Beige curtains, beige carpet, beige everything. Music seeped through from the day room; there were voices, laughter. Armchair aerobics. She dropped the tablecloths onto a chair, peeled off the top one, shook out the folds. With a flick of her wrists, the tablecloth billowed. She settled it on the table, flattened the creases with her palms, twisted it so the corners hung between the chairs. Turning, she noticed someone sitting at a table near the door. It was Vera, one of the residents, a recent arrival. Heather walked across, stood, looking down at her. She was small, bowed, her pink scalp visible through her white hair.

'You're keen, aren't you, Vera?' Heather said. 'Dinner isn't for another hour.'

Vera raised watery, red-rimmed eyes. She pressed a quavering smile, then looked down again, her swollen fingers fiddling with the hem of her polo-shirt.

Heather sank onto a chair. 'What's up?' She reached across and gently rubbed Vera's arm. Vera shook her head. 'Come on, you can tell me.' Heather leaned forward, peered up into Vera's face. She took hold of one of Vera's hands, squeezed it, stroked her wrist. 'Didn't you want to do your armchair aerobics?'

'Never thought I'd end up in a place like this,' Vera said quietly.

Heather felt the tears prickle, the tingle behind her nose. 'It's not that bad.' She squeezed Vera's hand again; so small, so fragile.

'Just hits you sometimes, you know.'

Heather nodded. In the day-room the music stopped; someone hooted.

'Never thought I'd be alone.'

'You're not alone really, are you?' Heather said. 'You've got lots of friends here.'

'They're not proper friends though, are they? They're just here. We're just here.'

'Of course they're friends. They're new friends, that's all. And anyway, you're my friend. I don't know where I'd be without you. Our chats make my day.'

Vera tried to smile. 'You're a good girl, Heather.'

Heather hung her head, laughed ruefully. 'I'm not sure about that.'

'Trust me, luvvie, you are. You've got a good heart.'

Heather stood. 'Right, come on, you. We can't have you moping about. If you're not going to do your armchair aerobics, you're just going to have to help me set these tables.'

Vera smiled up at her.

'Come on, up you get,' Heather chivvied, holding out a hand. 'You can earn your keep, young lady.'

A week later, Heather was alone in the clubhouse, sitting in the snug by the kitchen. She was browsing flats for rent on her phone, savouring the pictures, imagining herself in each room. She'd be able to afford something like that soon. Rain thrashed against the windows, gurgled in the drainpipe. She glanced up. Outside, beyond the empty car park, lights burned bright in the blurred bungalows across the road. The rain had settled in during the afternoon, had grown gradually heavier, keeping the golfers away.

She stood, walked across to the bar. The clock over the till read 6.45. She hadn't seen anyone for hours. Barbara had left at twelve; 'something important to do' she'd said; Victor was at some regional greenkeepers' meeting. Since going full-time, she'd noticed that neither of them ever actually did anything. And they were paid more than she was. How did that work? She stepped across to the till, pressed the button so it tallied the day's slim takings, the till roll rising, voluting. Her mobile phone buzzed. It was her dad again.

'We'll be in Pizza Express at 7.30. It'd be good if you could meet Sharon.' She deleted the message. Why wouldn't they just leave her alone? Her parents were both as bad. It was always one of them, expecting something from her. They'd been like that ever since they divorced. They were both completely selfish. And why would she care about her dad's new girlfriend? Anyway, she had another stack of ironing to do; she needed the money.

The till drawer sprang open. She tore off the printout, lifted out the cash tray and ferried it across to the bar. Reaching over to the wall by the sink, she flicked the switch so the striplight overhead buzzed, glowed at its extremities and coughed into life. She scooped out the pound coins, piling them in a mound, then looked across the sodden course. Hardly anyone had noticed that Tom had been sacked; that she'd taken his hours. Yesterday was the first time someone even mentioned it. Two of the old guys who played in the mornings, Harry and Ray, had come in for their post-round pint.

'What's this about Tom leaving?' Harry had asked.

'Left last week,' she'd said, handing over his change.

'Nice lad, Tom,' Ray said.

'So, what happened?' Harry persisted. She'd spotted that two of his lower teeth were missing.

'I don't think Barbara liked him,' she explained.

A low drone had swelled outside then Victor scudded past on his fairway mower.

'Wouldn't be surprised if he had something to do with it,' Harry said, nodding towards the greenkeeper.

'You'd better watch yourself, young 'un,' Ray had said,

carrying his glass across to a table in the dining area. 'They'll be after you next.'

And that's all anyone had said. She slid the coins into her palm, two at a time, counting the money.

★

Steam hissed from the iron as she laid the shirt sleeve flat on the board. Her phone buzzed. She picked it off the table, opened the text.

'Still at Pizza Express. Jack's here.' Jack was her half-brother, from her dad's second marriage. Music erupted from the room below, the bass boom throbbing up through the floor. The door next to her room slammed, the bolt snapped shut. Someone was in the toilet beyond the thin wall beside her bed. She slid the phone back onto the table then grasped the iron and tried not to listen.

As she smoothed the iron along the sleeve, pressing out the creases, she thought of Tom. For a moment she stared at the kettle on the fridge, then at her single bed. It was a shame for him, but a flat was going to cost her £700 a month. There were bills on top of that. Plus there was a deposit to find. No, she had to do what she had to do.

Beyond the wall, the toilet flushed, the bolt snapped back. She flipped over the sleeve, applied the iron. And she'd never said goodbye to Vera when she quit at the care home. But she had to get on, carve out a life for herself; no one was going to do it for her. Her phone was ringing. She leaned across, checked the number then made the connection.

'Hello, honey… Are you babe?' Trapping the phone to her ear with a shoulder, she positioned the shirt front, tugged it taut. 'Describe it to me…' Steam sighed from the iron.

The hot spell began in the last week of June. The fair weather rolled on, day after day, the sun baking the course, opening up long, wandering cracks in the earth.

From the shade of the clubhouse, Heather watched the couple recede down the fairway. She'd been working when it began. Barbara had been sitting at a table in the dining area, using her coloured pens to write up the previous week's takings for the treasurer's accounts. Simon had walked past her, swaggering splay-footed towards the bar.

'Any chance of a bacon roll?' he'd asked. Not even a please.

He'd pulled a note from his wallet, flipped it onto the bar.

'The kitchen's closed,' she'd said.

'I'll pay a bit extra if you open it for me.' He'd actually winked at her.

Barbara had glared across, scowling her sanction.

He was tapping at his phone when she deposited the sandwich on the bar. He'd taken a bite, nodded at the money and swiped the touch-screen. Didn't even look at her. 'How much for a game of golf?' he asked. She told him.

'Who's she?' he said, chewing, tilting his head towards Barbara.

'Clubhouse manager.'

He'd snatched a bite of his sandwich. 'A bit of all right, isn't she?'

Heather had shrugged, her lips twisting with distaste.

'Does she play?'

'You'll have to ask her.'

Simon had taken another bite of his sandwich. 'I will,' he said.

It had been going on for a month now, the relationship, or whatever it was. Barbara talked about it all the time, graphically. It was nauseating. He was an estate manager at a London banker's country pile, lived in the grounds with his girlfriend.

Beyond Barbara and Simon, in the further distance, players trekked a far fairway, small figures against the wood-swathed hillside rising behind them. More players were hiking down the second fairway. The course was full again.

'Yes, please, Heather.' She hadn't heard Victor enter. He was hitching onto a barstool.

After pouring his drink she wandered across to the patio door, stood there, the warm draught whispering across her.

Victor was crouching forward over his half-full glass, picking at a raw blond gouge in the wooden bar-top. 'She out there with Simon?'

'Mmm…'

'People are noticing.' He turned, rested the glass on his knee.

'What, that she never does any work?' She bent to scratch an itch on her leg. When she straightened, she saw Victor trying to peek down her vest-top. Caught in the act, he smiled, then sipped his drink.

'Well, she doesn't, does she?' she said. 'I mean, what does she actually do?'

Victor snickered, his head ducking.

'Mainly she's out there playing golf or she's with Simon.' She took a step towards Victor, stalled. There was a stench lingering around him, a melange of accumulated body odour and the fungal tang of clothes left too long in the washing machine. Heather retreated to the doorway again. 'Do the members know he's married?'

Victor laughed. 'They only live together.' He guzzled another mouthful of lager.

'Do they know?' Heather watched him.

He shrugged, rubbed his chin, the rough rasp of his stubble audible, then stood, arching his back, stretching. 'I don't suppose she'd have spread it about.' He brushed past her, stepped out onto the sun-soaked patio and sat on a bench.

'People wouldn't really mind though, would they?' She leaned her shoulder against the plastic door-jamb, folded her arms.

'Some would,' he said.

'Like who?'

'Well, Beth, for one.' Victor sipped his lager.

Heather waited.

'Husband went off with a barmaid.'

'Really?' Heather smiled, widened her eyes. Figures were rounding the eighteenth fairway's dog-leg, moving into their homeward approach. 'Who else?'

Victor drained his glass, held it up towards her. 'Yes please, Heather.'

Heather stepped out into the molten sunlight, shading her eyes with a hand. 'Who else wouldn't like it?'

The after-work crowd had begun returning to the clubhouse at 7.30, drifting back in groups. Most of them were in now, had bought their drinks. Some had settled out on the patio to enjoy the evening sun, others were relaxing in the shade of the clubhouse. Their conversations rolled, fragments erupting from the hum.

'…told me it was diabetes…'

'…I prefer the Slazenger…'

'…and she just kept crapping on about grebes…'

'Victor!' a voice outside called. A group was walking from the eighteenth green towards the clubhouse. Victor was still out on the patio.

Heather thumbed the soft drinks gun, filled two glasses with sizzling soda. 'That's two pounds, please, Nigel.'

Nigel mined his pocket for change then examined the coins on his palm. Broad-shouldered, stub-nosed and silver-haired, he was the current vice-captain. In his fifties, Heather guessed. He handed across the correct change. 'What time did

Victor start drinking today?' He lifted the glasses, took a sip from one.

She shrugged, smiling, then turned to the till as he moved away.

'...the truss doesn't help...'

'...still think we'd be better in Europe...'

'...keep having to push it back in with my finger...'

'Now then, Heather,' Brian said, arriving at the bar. Small, and with a pencil-thin moustache, he was a town councillor.

'How are you, Brian?' she asked, planting her hands on her hips.

'Oh, on the crest of a slump, thank you, Heather,' he said lavishly, then placed his order.

As she filled the first glass, a taller, affluent-looking man arrived at Brian's side. She didn't recognise him. She lifted the glass onto the bar, beer slopping over the side, pooling at its base. She was filling the next glass when Nigel's voice drifted in.

'Have you actually done anything today? The greens are shit, Victor.'

'There you go,' she said, delivering the drink.

Brian proffered a twenty-pound note. Heather returned the change then watched the two men wander towards an empty table over by the cigarette machine.

'...can get a trade deal quite easily...'

'...young people don't want to do those jobs...'

'...it'll be fine now we've got Boris...'

She turned. Victor stumbled into the clubhouse, caught his balance. Swaying slightly, he lifted his chin, wagged it at the room, then listed towards the fruit machine and hunkered onto a bar stool in the corner. Heather set a glass to fill under the lager tap, looked along the clubhouse. Barbara was tacking through the crowd with Simon in tow.

'I don't know why I bother,' Victor slurred disconsolately. He was fixing Heather with glazed, sorrowful eyes, his chin raised meaningfully. 'Have you any idea what it's like?' She placed the pint on the bar in front of him. 'The ingratitude I've got to deal with…' he shook his head. 'Thirty-four years I've given this place…' He took a sip. '…Thirty-four years. And I get treated like this… After everything I've sacrificed…'

Barbara was beside Victor now. Behind her, Simon fed coins into the slot machine, slapped the button.

'A pint of lager and a small lemonade,' Barbara requested, then pivoted away.

'No idea what I do for this place,' Victor said towards the space Barbara had lately occupied, turning as he spoke. He hitched round further, fell silent. Barbara was pressing herself into Simon's back. She pushed her hands into his pockets and rummaged. Victor leaned forward, craning for a better view.

Reaching down for a glass, Heather noticed Nigel in the doorway, watching the scene. He shook his head, disbelievingly. 'Enjoying the show, Victor?' Nigel called, rolling his eyes at Heather.

She laughed noiselessly as Victor swivelled away. He

bumped his elbow onto the bar, leaned a cheek on his hand, and stared sullenly across the golf course. Outside, the late sun lit the air gold; the trees cast dense, attenuated shadows.

*

The hot spell continued into July.

Another long morning was unfurling. The heat had already risen and become oppressive. The air seeping into the clubhouse was humid, tangible. A couple of flies zipped angularly above the bar as the resonant hammer of a woodpecker at work drifted in from the tall trees beyond Victor's bungalow.

There were only the ladies out on the course. Three of them. Heather stepped out onto the patio, the ice clinking in her glass. The sun hadn't travelled round yet so the patio remained doused in shade. And Barbara was off with Simon again, another seedy assignation, probably. Heather leaned her shoulder against the wall. Along the seared 18th fairway the course had crusted up, turned brown. The heat was already warping the light, causing a shimmer across the earth's surface. Why should she be left to do all the work?

The ladies returned to the clubhouse just before one o'clock. They were sitting at a table on the patio, sheltering beneath a parasol, its fringe brushing the wall of the clubhouse.

Heather lowered the tray to the table.

'Thank you, Heather,' Pam said, distributing the cups and saucers. She was small, grey-haired, had birdlike movements.

'Shall I be mother?' Susan asked, leaning forward, lifting the teapot. Her hair was stringently bobbed, dyed blond; she wore glasses.

'Can I get you anything else?' Heather asked, backing towards the door.

'No, thank you, Heather,' Susan said, tipping tea into one cup, then the next, holding down the lid of the teapot as she poured.

'Maybe you could help us with one thing, though,' Beth said, smiling. She was thin, red-haired, had a dimpled chin. Resting her elbows on the arm of the chair, she interlocked her fingers under her chin.

'If I can,' Heather volunteered.

'We were talking, and we were wondering about Barbara,' Beth said.

'A lot of people have been wondering about Barbara,' Susan contributed.

'Where is she?' Pam asked, turning jerkily. She was the current ladies' captain.

'I'm not sure,' Heather equivocated.

'Hmm…' Pam nodded.

'With this new fella of hers?' Beth prompted.

'Mmm…' Heather said. The sun had moved round now, its light clipping the edge of the patio.

'Been making quite a performance out of it, we hear,'

Susan said. She reached for the milk jug, dribbled some into her cup, offered it across to Pam.

'Who is he?' Beth asked.

'An estate manager somewhere, I think. Simon.'

Beth nodded, then levelled her eyes at Heather, waiting.

'Lives on the grounds with his girlfriend,' Heather added. 'I think she takes care of the stables.'

'Does she?' Beth nodded slowly, a muscle twitching in her jaw. Susan and Pam exchanged glances. 'Does this girlfriend know about Barbara?'

Heather raised a hand to her throat. 'Have I said the wrong thing?'

'Of course not,' Pam cooed, soothingly.

'I don't want to get Barbara into trouble.'

'You won't get Barbara into trouble,' Pam said.

'We're just curious, that's all,' Susan said.

Heather smiled apologetically.

'Does his girlfriend know?' Beth repeated, more firmly this time.

'I don't think so.'

'No,' Beth said, 'she wouldn't, would she?' Beth looked at Susan.

Susan crooked an eyebrow, sat back, resting the saucer on her blue-veined thigh. 'Would you mind if we pay when we finish?' she asked casually.

Heather hesitated, touched her cheek. 'You won't say I said anything, will you?'

'Thank you, Heather,' Pam said, lifting her saucer and hitching back in her chair.

*

It happened ten days later, on a sweltering Saturday evening.

A few members lingered on in the bar, wearing their green club blazers, their faces florid with afternoon sun and the post-meal vinous flush. Brian Nash was sitting at the bar with Nigel standing beside him. Brian chortled appreciatively at something Nigel said.

Sweat beaded in Heather's hairline then trickled down her temple. She was washing glasses in the sink; the glass-wash machine was broken again. Why should she always be the one to clear up? Barbara hadn't even offered an excuse this time; she'd just dashed off as soon as she'd finished dishing up the pudding. On her way to meet Simon, presumably. Someone gently touched her forearm.

'Thanks for today, Heather.' It was Frank Watson, the captain, leaning through into the bar. His stubble had darkened, become crepuscular. 'Everything was perfect.'

'It was a pleasure, Frank,' she said, smiling wearily.

Beyond Frank, in the clubhouse, the shadows were creeping from their corners, reclaiming the room. She dragged her wrist across her forehead.

'Right then, chaps. Let's get you home,' Frank said.

'Night, Victor,' she heard Brian say.

She turned. Victor was back. He'd been drinking all day. Since the sun had begun to sink, he'd been intermittently driving off on the buggy, shifting the sprinkler from green to green. He was standing beside Nigel now, a finger sapiently crooked against his lips.

Brian stood, fed his shirt into the waistband of his slacks.

She dried her hands on a tea towel, watched the men weave among the tables.

'Yes, please, Heather,' Victor slurred. His hips were in perpetual motion, moving elastically as he fought for control. Above the brim of his cap there was a white salt stain.

'What do you want, Victor?' Heather asked sharply.

He clacked his tongue, thoughtfully.

After she'd poured his drink, she followed him as he carried his glass outside. She needed some fresh air. And she needed to sit down; her legs ached. She sank onto a low table. The sun had long slipped below the tree line; the day's embers were fading, the sky's blue deepening. Gathered heat seeped from the brickwork; the plastic gutters emitted short, sharp cracks as they contracted. Bats were flitting overhead; blackbirds murmured, nesting down.

'Don't realise how much I do,' Victor mumbled. 'Still working now,' he shrugged, sticking out his bottom lip.

Heather shifted. She felt sticky, uncomfortable. It had been a long day.

They both heard the car door slam out in the car park. She kicked off a flip-flop, rested her foot on her knee and massaged her sole, manipulating the aching instep. The floorboards groaned in the clubhouse. She tried to peer through the window but could only see her own reflection, her sweat-frizzed hair. Then Barbara's outline was occupying the doorway.

Victor sipped his cider, glanced up, white-eyed.

'Everything all right, Barbara?' Heather asked. Barbara's shoulders were shaking. Heather stood, the flagstones warm beneath her bare feet. 'What's wrong?' She stepped across. 'Come on, come and sit down.' She touched Barbara's elbow, shepherded her to the bench and sat her beside Victor. Heather perched on the edge of the table opposite. 'Do you want to talk about it?'

Barbara slumped back, lost in thought.

Heather considered the ragged cut across the bridge of Barbara's nose. Under her eyes, bruising had started to colour. Heather glanced at Victor. He was studying Barbara sidelong.

'What's happened, Barbara?' Heather leaned forward, folded her arms onto her knees. Victor was staring down her vest-top again but she couldn't be bothered to move.

'Someone told her. Wrote her a letter.'

Victor drained his glass, stood, tottered into the clubhouse, sinking into the shadow. Glasses chattered. Heather lifted her foot again, rubbed her sole.

'Told who?' Heather asked.

'Simon's girlfriend. She must have followed him.' Barbara banged her head back against the wall, angled her face to the sky. 'Oh, God.'

Victor stumbled out onto the patio. He held a tumbler of whisky towards Barbara. 'Make you feel better,' he said, handing her the glass. He sat heavily, sipped his cider.

'What happened?' Heather prompted.

'She was waiting outside the hotel…'

Victor lifted a finger to his lips, his mouth twitching into a smile.

'…been sitting there all afternoon.'

'What happened to your face?'

'Punched me. Right there in the car park.'

Victor sniggered. Heather glowered at him.

'Mmm, curious the circle that turns,' he said sagely, trying not to smirk.

Heather's mouth opened, she shook her head. She looked back at Barbara. 'What happened then?'

'He went off with her.'

Heather gazed down at the flagstones, scrunched her toes, gripping the grittiness. 'So it's over then?'

'He turned up at mine an hour ago. Blind drunk. He's left her. Said he's quitting his job so we can start a new life together.' Barbara closed her eyes.

'Is that what you want?'

Barbara didn't reply. Heather stared at the split across her nose. She'd definitely have two black eyes in the morning.

'I don't know how to tell you this, Barbara,' Heather said softly, 'but somehow all the members know about you and

Simon. Not everyone's all that happy about it.'

Barbara vented a long, low groan, knocked her head back against the wall again.

Heather widened her eyes at Victor, nodded encouragingly.

'Sometimes we all need new beginnings,' Victor said. 'Look at me...'

'What are you going to do?' Heather interrupted.

'What can I do?' Barbara raised the glass to her lips, sipped.

Heather squinted into the clubhouse. Well, there was still the cleaning...

The weather broke a few days later.

Heather stood at the bar, tallying the previous week's takings on a sheet of paper. With the club phone trapped to her ear, she slid the sheet of paper back into the plastic wallet, hooked it into the ring binder, snapped the clasp shut.

'Yes, I'd like to place the order for Sudleigh Golf Club, please... Yep, sure...'

Colin was walking towards the bar. He was the new employee, an acquaintance of Victor's, late forties, greying hair, a bankrupted ex-publican. She ignored him.

'Yep, can we have three London Pride, three Carling, two Guinness, and a Magners.' She placed the calculator on top of the folder. 'No, we'll get that from the cash and carry...' She swapped the phone to her other ear. 'Well, it's cheaper... Yep, that's everything. That's great. Yep...OK. Thanks, bye.' She lifted the phone from her ear, pushed it along the bar.

'Morning, Heather,' Colin said. He was standing behind her somewhere. She didn't turn.

'Colin.' She lifted the folder, tucked it under her arm.

'All quiet on the Western Front?'

'Right, I've got to go.' She picked her bag from the barstool, slipped her arm through the strap, paused. 'You haven't done those blinds yet,' she said.

'It was pretty busy yesterday.'

'Well it isn't today, so maybe you could do them now. Just give them a wipe down. Get rid of that dust.' She hoisted her bag.

Colin was staring at the blinds.

'Anyway, I'd better be off,' she said. 'I've got a rep coming in this afternoon from the local radio. Something about advertising.'

'For this tin-pot shit-hole?'

She inhaled sharply. 'If you could just get those blinds done.' She strode quickly along the clubhouse.

Outside, she unlocked the car door, wrenched it open, slung her bag and folder onto the passenger seat, then climbed in. She slammed the door shut, started the engine.

As she ground the stick into gear, she peered out of the window at the sag-roofed clubhouse, at Victor's prefab bungalow beside it. The bungalow's once-white walls were streaked a mossy green. Was it just a tin-pot shit-hole after all?

The summer had gradually ebbed away. Autumn had crept in as August passed.

Rain was beating hard against the windows; the early September squall scoured the fairways, ripping leaves from the trees. There was no one out on the course, only Victor mowing his lonely fairways. And he probably wasn't actually out there. He'd be sheltering in the shed. Or, more likely, he'd be back at home, drinking.

With little to do, these had become long days. Heather turned the page of *The Sudleigh Gazette*. Theft from garden sheds. Brawl outside a town-centre pub. An am-dram write-up. She flipped the page again, began to skim the recruitment section for situations vacant. Lowering her head, she read more carefully.

'Estate agent sales consultant. Full training given.'

Having been manager of a golf club would look impressive on her CV. She could see herself as an estate agent. And the money would be better. She stood, folded the newspaper. She would use the computer in the office.

MIRIAM

She'd only just come home after her yoga class.

The lazy October light flowed in through the French windows. Over the last few days a soft heat had returned. Miriam took a drink from her water bottle and considered the kitchen table, the clear plastic folder containing worksheets and a notepad. Her Spanish homework. It had to be done by Friday's class and it was Tuesday already. Next door's washing machine rumbled faintly, beginning its spin cycle. She took another long sip of water, then, as she screwed on the bottle top, the doorbell chimed.

She breezed out of the kitchen and through the lounge. In the small entrance hall, she unlocked the front door, pulled it open. Lydia was standing on the pavement. She was wearing large sunglasses.

'You ready then?' Lydia asked. Cars lined the street behind her; sunlight glittered in the upper windows of the terraced houses opposite.

'Ready for what?'

'The show home. I've booked an appointment.'

While they were driving to Wisley on Sunday, Lydia had been complaining about the glut of local building, especially that new estate at the top of town. Miriam had suggested they view the show home sometime, to see what it was like.

'Let me get changed,' Miriam protested. 'I've just got in.'

'You'll be fine,' Lydia said. 'If we go now we can miss the school traffic.'

★

They strolled through the brick-and-flint gateposts. Six pink-roofed houses were clustered round a brief stretch of unmarked road. Beyond lay the remains of a field, stripped and levelled; after that woodland took over, climbing the hillside.

They advanced up the show home's block-paved driveway. A large wooden hoarding emblazoned with the developer's name dominated the meagre front garden.

'We're a bit early,' Miriam observed.

Lydia removed her sunglasses. 'It'll be fine,' she said and palmed open the front door.

Miriam followed her into the hallway. Light channelled

through from the bright kitchen at the end of the corridor, but it was still a dark space. There were voices leaking out from the lounge to the right. 'It's the perfect choice for a first-time buyer,' someone was saying.

Miriam surveyed the decor. Grey walls, pale blue carpet, white ceiling and skirtings.

'It's not very big,' Lydia said, opening the under-stairs cupboard.

A young woman appeared in the lounge doorway. She was wearing a black skirt and blazer. 'Heather,' her name-badge stated.

'Hello, ladies,' she said, clamping her hands together. 'Can I help?'

Miriam pressed the light switch. Overhead the bulb kindled.

'We're the three o'clock,' Lydia said, turning as she closed the cupboard. 'Dixon,' she added.

'Sorry, but I'm actually with a client...' Heather began.

'Don't let us stop you,' Lydia cut in, raising a hand. 'We'll show ourselves round.' Spinning away, she struck for the kitchen.

Miriam pushed her bag straps up her shoulder and followed.

After a brief inspection of the kitchen, they scaled the stairs. Miriam investigated the master bedroom at the rear while Lydia explored elsewhere. There were built-in wardrobes, a bed with a TV that rose from the foot-end. She moved towards the window. Outside, a scrap of lawn was trapped between tall fences. In a far corner of the field, diggers were at work, quietly excavating. There were footfalls behind her.

'Don't get much for your money, do you?' Lydia said. She knocked on a hollow-sounding partition wall, then wafted out again.

'I wouldn't want to live here,' Miriam said, peering down at the garden. The turf hadn't yet knitted, the borders were bare.

A sound drew her attention. Her phone was ringing. She opened her tote bag, retrieved her mobile. It was Jason, her son. She frowned at the screen for a moment, then dropped the phone back into her bag and wandered out onto the landing.

Lydia emerged from the bathroom. 'If you bought it you'd never sell it,' she said, sauntering past. She stalled at the top of the stairs. 'Fancy grabbing a coffee somewhere?'

'I should really start my Spanish.'

'Bueno,' Lydia said and began her descent.

In Miriam's bag, her mobile beeped.

★

Miriam locked the front door, toed off her trainers. She barefooted through the lounge, passed the crowded bookcase, the stairs. Settling her bag on the kitchen table, she delved and pulled out her mobile. There was a text message.

'It's Jason. Can you call me back. It's important.'

She walked across, slid her phone onto the oak worktop,

then picked a key from the terracotta dish by the kettle. She unlocked the back door, hauled it open. There were shrieks from her neighbour's garden; the children playing on the trampoline. She stepped out onto the narrow patio and paused, the concrete slabs warm underfoot. A low drone began beyond the back fence; someone mowing their lawn in the next street along.

She scanned the run of rosebushes down the right-hand border, their second flush wearying now. At the end, the fuchsias were still in flower, though the clematis by the shed had finished for the year.

Closing her eyes, she angled her face up to the sun. She would have to call Jason. But it was always so difficult with him. He'd never forgiven her for walking out on the family just after he started at Sudleigh College. She'd tried keeping in touch, had tried to explain, but he'd never wanted to listen, had done his best to avoid her. The last time she'd seen him was in a Haslemere coffee shop, five years ago. They'd talked about his job, his new flat. She'd only said how proud she was, and he suddenly shifted gear.

'Do you think it was worth it?' he'd said, from nowhere.

She'd looked at him, uncertain.

'You walking out on us.'

'It wasn't like that,' she'd said.

'Well, you seem OK now.'

She hadn't known what he was talking about.

'Are you still taking the tablets?'

'What tablets?'

'For the mental illness thing.'

'Mental illness?' she'd asked, and then it had dawned on her. 'I don't know what your dad's been telling you but I'm not the one with a problem.'

'Don't try and put this on Dad,' he fired back. 'You were the one that left.'

She hadn't argued, hadn't offered a defence. What would have been the point? He'd never wanted to know how his dad had treated her; didn't want to hear her side of the story.

Blinking open her eyes, she tracked a plane's slow progress across the deep blue sky. It was all so long ago; fourteen years since she left. She'd built a new life in that time. Perhaps they'd all moved on, changed. She watched the vapour trail loosen and unravel, listened to the children play.

After a while she heard the ringtone of her mobile issuing from the kitchen. It would be Jason again, she knew. She turned, stepped back into the house. Then, inhaling sharply, she scooped up her phone and swiped to connect.

'Hello?' she said, padding across the kitchen and into the lounge.

'I've been trying to get hold of you.'

'I've been busy.' She approached the bay window. Shadows were climbing the red-brick house-front opposite. A Union flag filled an upstairs window.

'I didn't know if you'd answer.' He sounded just like his father.

Miriam ran her tongue round her teeth. 'So, how are you, Jason?'

'Oh, you know...'

'Are you still...' She'd forgotten what he did. It was IT-related. 'In Guildford?'

'I'm based in Winchester now.'

'Oh...' She tried to think of something else to say. 'And how's Claire?'

'She's fine.'

She watched a car slide by.

'Well, it's good of you to ring,' she said, eventually.

'Anyway,' he began, 'the reason I'm calling...' There was a pause. 'It's about Dad.'

Miriam raised her eyebrows and waited.

'He's going into hospital on Monday. A triple bypass...' He hesitated, then spoke quickly. 'He said he'd like to see you.'

'Pardon?'

'I'm just passing on the message. But I think there are some things he'd like to say.'

'Like what?' she said, incredulous.

Silence flowed down the line.

'And what about Janet? Isn't she going to mind?' Janet was the woman Greg, her ex, had lived with for the past eight years. Miriam had heard about it from her old friends in Guildford.

'She's moved to Cornwall.'

'Has she,' Miriam said, a smile in her voice.

'I just think he wants to make peace.'

'Make peace?' Shaking her head, she turned and paced into the kitchen.

'He only wants to talk to you.'

'Well, I don't want to talk to him.' She stood by the table, gripped the back of a chair.

'Couldn't you just do it for my sake?'

She looked along the garden. A pair of industrious blackbirds were probing the lawn for worms.

'Look, I haven't asked anything from you over the years, have I?'

She screwed her eyes shut, bowed her head.

'Please?' he insisted.

'Right. OK.' She stared at the table-top, the folder containing her homework.

'Have you got his number?'

She bridled. 'Why would I have his number?'

'For God's sake. It was just a question.'

'OK, fine.' She stalked across the kitchen, took a pen and pad from beside the microwave in the corner. 'Right, what is it?

She scrawled the number.

'And you'll go and see him?'

'I didn't say I'd see him, Jason.'

'Please?'

'I've said I'll phone him, haven't I?'

'All right. So when are you going call? Then I can let him know.'

'Jesus, Jason,' she snapped.

'What about tomorrow?'

'Fine. I'll ring him tomorrow then.'

A silence opened. She went and stood at the back door. The blackbirds took flight, skimming away over the back fence.

'Look, I'm sorry to do this...'

'Right,' she said slowly, knowingly.

'It's just I've a meeting at five.'

'Of course you do.'

'OK,' he said. 'I've got to go.' The call ended.

She skidded the phone across the worktop, looked at it for a moment, then stepped out onto the patio. The sun was dipping toward the roof-line across the back, lighting a brilliant stripe along the upper half of the right-hand fence. Next door the children had gone in; crockery clattered in their kitchen. Miriam drew a deep breath, the air soft and sweet with the smell of freshly-cut grass. She shouldn't have answered the phone; should have left things as they were. Remote. It was easier that way. The bronzing leaves of the neighbour's birch rustled in the breeze. Exhaling heavily, she set off along the lawn, the grass soft under her soles.

At end of the garden, she unbolted the shed door, let it fall open on its sagging hinges. Reaching in, she picked her secateurs from a shelf and wandered back towards the house. She stalled, contemplating the rose bush nearest the patio, its soft pink flowers browning at the edges here and there. Why should she speak to Greg again? After the things he'd done.

She'd spent years burying it all. She felt her chest tighten, the anger rising now.

She thumbed the secateurs' safety catch and stepped forward. Crouching, she stared down at the dark soil. There was the way she hadn't been allowed friends, or a life even.

'I know you're having an affair,' Greg would say when she came in from work. She'd been a receptionist at the hospital, in the oncology department, after Jason started school.

'I'm not, Greg,' she'd protest. But he wouldn't let it go.

'Tell me who he is.' And it would escalate from there; threats, demands for divorce.

Then he started turning up at work, making accusations, shouting in reception. She'd had to resign in the end. That's how it always was. She couldn't have anything of her own.

She singled out a rose stalk, clipped it off and dropped it onto the lawn behind her. Kneeling, the cool earth damp through her trousers, she pushed her greying hair out of her face with the back of her wrist. She selected another stem, nipped it off near the base. She was still out there working after the sun had slumped behind the houses beyond the back fence.

*

In the doctor's surgery, behind the reception's plastic screens, Miriam stopped typing. She sat back, her chair creaking.

'So we went and had a look at that new Waitrose,' Debbie

said, hidden behind her monitor. She'd been talking for a while. 'Didn't think it was that special...'

Miriam contemplated the mobile phone beside her keyboard. Yes, she would have to call Greg. For Jason's sake. She should just get it over with.

'...not that much choice, really. And it's expensive. Pete said he preferred Lidl.'

'Do you fancy a cuppa?' Miriam said, snatching her mobile from the desk and standing suddenly.

Debbie looked up. She was blond-haired, blue-eyed, would soon be forty-eight. She'd been working there just over a month. 'It's my turn, isn't it?'

'Give us your cup.' Miriam stifled a yawn as she held out her hand.

'You tired, Miriam?' Debbie said, passing her mug over the monitors.

'Didn't get much sleep.'

'I've told you before. It's all that running round you do with those clubs and classes.'

The office phone was ringing again. It had hardly stopped all morning.

'You should think about yourself a bit more.' Debbie reached for the handset, lifted it to her ear. 'Hello, Broadlands Surgery,' she said, putting on her posh voice. 'Oh, hello Miss Bennett... Let's just check... That's right. Yes, this Friday...'

Miriam crossed to the security door, twisted the latch. She strode through into the waiting room. There was only one patient in, a weathered young woman who was absently scratching her arm as she studied the floor. Miriam continued along the corridor, passing the closed doors of the doctors' consulting rooms, the punctuating pot plants, palms and ferns, the nurse's room. Rounding the corner, she pushed through the swing door into the kitchen.

Dr Hugh was by the sink. His shoulders hunched, he was rubbing his face with both hands. There was the faint fizz of his eleven o'clock Solpadeine dissolving in a glass of water.

'Hello, Hugh,' Miriam said, drifting over to the window. A haze still hung in the air outside, remnants of the morning's mist that hadn't yet burned away. She listened to Hugh rinse his glass, place it on the draining board.

'Should get back,' he said ruefully.

She turned and watched the door close behind him. For a moment she considered the phone in her hand, then she dropped it into her pocket and walked across to the sink. She placed the cups in the washing up bowl, filled the kettle, returned it to the worktop and switched it on. She gazed out towards the ice-blue sky for a moment. Yes, she would phone Greg later, after her art class. The kettle crackled into life and she set the hot tap running to wash the cups.

*

Light washed in through the long windows behind them, slanting viscous beams across the Community Centre's garden room. They were doing mountains today. Sean had just finished his demonstration.

'And remember,' Sean said, 'this is an exercise in proportion and atmospheric perspective. And don't forget to let the paint dry before you start the next layer. OK,' he clapped his hands resonantly, 'over to you.'

Miriam was sitting at the last easel in the arc. Lydia was at the easel beside her.

'Are you going to phone him then?' Lydia said, blending paints in the lid of her watercolour tin. Miriam had told her about the Jason situation while they waited for Sean to arrive.

Miriam chose a broad brush from the bundle on the table. 'I don't know,' she murmured, rubbing the soft bristles against her palm.

'Did he say to start with the sky?' Lydia peered over at the next student's canvas. 'That's what Andrea's doing,' she confided.

The light across Miriam's back was warm, soothing. She stared at the blank canvas and listened to the faint thump of a beat seep through from the room next door. The Dancing for Fitness class had begun.

Lydia had been applying a peculiar brown backwash. She stepped back and leaned her head on one side, assessing her work. 'Do you want to open it all up again?' she asked.

Miriam mixed a touch of turquoise with some cerulean hue. 'I'm just surprised Jason phoned. I mean, maybe he's starting to see things differently.'

Lydia rinsed her brush in the jar of water, the ferrule rattling against the sides. 'Not everyone can change,' she mused.

Miriam sniffed. 'So, how's it going with Tony?' Lydia and Tony's was an on-off relationship. They were currently 'trying again,' with Lydia staying over at Tony's a few nights a week.

Lydia stabbed her bristles into the burnt sienna. 'Don't get me started about Tony.'

Miriam swept her brush across the canvas with smooth, languid strokes.

'Did I tell you about my idea?' Lydia said, changing the subject.

'What's that?' Miriam swirled her brush in the jar, the clear water clouding.

'We should run an In Bloom entry. To bring people together.'

Miriam glanced across, saw she was serious.

'So how are we getting on over here?' Sean said, arriving between their easels.

'It has a certain energy,' Lydia stated, matter-of-factly.

'We are concentrating, aren't we, ladies?' Sean said, smiling.

'Absolutely,' Lydia confirmed, nodding.

'And it's important that we let other people focus too.' Sean held up a hand and backed away.

Miriam smiled at him then combined a little yellow ochre with her blue.

'What do you think then?' Lydia whispered. 'About In Bloom?'

Miriam frowned at her meaningfully then tried to gauge where the first ridge of peaks belonged.

★

She hadn't gone for coffee after class, had told Lydia she needed to finish her Spanish.

Sitting at the kitchen table, her notepad and worksheets spread in front of her, Miriam studied the French windows. The sunlight through the leaves of next door's birch was throwing shadows onto the glass. She looked down at her pad, read over what she'd written.

'*Me llamo Miriam. Vivo en Sudleigh. Tengo cincuenta y seis años. Estoy divorciada. Tengo un hijo. Se llama Jason.*'

She slouched back, gazing at her pocket dictionary. How could she speak to Greg? After the way he'd treated her. Like how he'd erupt, shouting and throwing things if she said something he didn't like.

But when Jason had started at college, the situation grew worse. On the day she left, she'd been cutting bread for Greg's sandwiches.

He'd been watching her. 'Can you do that any slower?' he said.

'You can do it yourself if you're not happy with the service,' she replied. That's all it took. He'd flown across the kitchen and grabbed her by the throat, pushing her back over the sink.

'You're hurting me, Greg,' she said.

He'd pushed her back even harder, his grip tightening. 'And what are you going to do about it?'

She'd still had the bread knife in her hand, had raised it slightly, defiantly.

He'd glanced down. 'Go on then,' he goaded. 'I dare you.'

It had been another of those mornings she'd cried after he left for work. But she'd known then that she could have happily stuck the knife right into him. And that's when she'd packed a bag.

The shadows shifted on the glass. No, she didn't want to speak to Greg. And she didn't want to think about those times. They were the past. She laid her pencil down on her pad and slowly stood, careful not to drag the tablecloth with her. Crossing to the back door, she stepped outside and set off towards the shed.

*

'I just don't like to think of you being lonely,' Debbie said, the keys clattering as she typed.

Miriam leaned down and hoisted her tote bag onto the desk.

'You should try a dating website. It's how I met Pete.'

Miriam pursed her lips thoughtfully. Was that everything? She'd called Mr Thompson and asked him to come in about his cholesterol; she'd done the repeat prescriptions, updated the appointments for next week. She'd even re-arranged the magazines and watered all the plants.

'It's dead simple,' Debbie said. 'You just put in what type of man you're looking for.'

Miriam stood, lifted her jacket from the back of the chair.

'I put in that I wanted someone kind and intelligent.'

Miriam pushed an arm into a jacket sleeve. 'And it came up with Pete?'

'Well, there were three or four local ones, but Pete looked the kindest.'

Shouldering her bag, Miriam noticed a man waiting at the reception counter.

'Honestly, it's so easy. You should think about it.'

'Can you get this?' Miriam tilted her head toward the reception desk. 'I've got to go.'

Debbie stood. 'What is it this afternoon? Spanish or something?

'That's tomorrow. The gentleman, Debbie.'

Debbie ambled towards the counter, the plastic slats clacked open. 'Can I help?'

Miriam hurried through the waiting room. Someone coughed. A toddler at the front was straining to break free from his reins, reaching for the magazines on the table. She passed through the sliding doors as the first wail erupted.

The wind was gusting across the car-park. It had shifted direction overnight, bringing the sharp autumn air. She unlocked her car, climbed in, swung the door shut. Looking in the rear-view mirror, she organised her fringe, tucked her bobbed hair behind her ears, and met her own grey-eyed gaze. No, she wasn't going to phone Greg. She didn't owe him a thing. And her Spanish homework was more pressing. It had to be finished by tomorrow.

Bending forwards, she glanced up at the heavy clouds, then pushed the key into the ignition and started the engine.

*

Outside, the day had faded. Intermittently, rain blew against the French windows. With her elbows on the kitchen table, the light bright overhead, Miriam read back over her homework.

'Me llamo Miriam. Tengo cincuenta y seis años. Vivo en Sudleigh. Soy recepcionista. Vivo solo porque estoy divorciada...' She smiled, pleased with the sentence construction. *'...Tengo un hijo. Se llama Jason. Está casado con Claire. Viven en Haslemere...'*

She glanced at the tablecloth, the shreds of eraser swept aside after all her corrections. What else could she say? I love gardening. I love my garden would be easier. Or I like to garden. What was the verb 'to garden'?

She was riffling through her pocket dictionary when the doorbell's chime cut through the silence. It chimed again.

'All right,' Miriam muttered, standing, pushing back her chair. If this was Lydia about her In Bloom master-plan...

She hurried through the house, flicked on the light in the vestibule and unlocked the front door, wrenched it open. A tall shirt-sleeved man was standing on the doorstep, his back to her. His broad shoulders were raised against the rain.

Miriam felt her throat tighten. 'Hello, Jason,' she said. 'Do you want to come in?'

He turned, pressed a tight smile and lowered his eyes. 'I can't stop,' he said, advancing.

She backed into the lounge. As he pushed the door shut, she moved through to the kitchen. 'Can I get you something?' she called, looking back along the house. 'A cup of tea? A towel?'

Jason prowled towards her, his head down. His shirt was sticking to his skin in places. 'I'm fine, thanks,' he said. It was only the second time he'd visited.

'It's good to see you, Jason.' She retreated, bumped back against the worktop's edge. 'So how's everything with you?' she asked, folding her arms.

He was scanning the shelf above the sink, the bits she'd collected on her holidays, shells from Cornwall, an egg-cup from Norwich, a dish from a pottery in Yorkshire. She could see Greg in his features, the nose, the eyes.

He met her gaze. 'So you haven't phoned Dad, then.'

She slowly shook her head. 'I couldn't, Jason.' She saw him glance at the table, her Spanish homework. 'I'm learning Spanish,' she said, raising a hand, holding her throat.

Jason rubbed through his short-cropped hair. 'You said you'd phone him.'

'It's not that simple.'

He squinted at her, disbelieving.

'I can't do it,' she said. 'I won't let him in again.'

'It's just a phone call.' There was suppressed anger in his voice.

'Look, Jason, there are things I never told you.'

His eyes hardened. 'Please don't,' he said, shaking his head. 'I've only come to see if you'll ring him.'

'I don't think you realise what you're asking.'

'You know,' he smiled sadly, 'I thought you might have changed.'

'Me?' she said, staring at him.

'But it's always about you, isn't it?'

A vast, aching hollowness opened inside her. 'That's just not true,' she said, her voice quavering. 'You've no idea what he was like. You didn't see. He was clever.'

Jason was shaking his head again. 'He said you'd do this. Start telling your stories.'

'Stories?' Colour rose to her cheeks. 'He was cruel, Jason. And he enjoyed it.'

Jason turned, as though to leave.

'I had to get out,' she insisted. 'There wasn't an option.'

He hung his head and slowly massaged his eyelids.

She leaned forward. 'I did try to keep in touch with you. I really did.'

'So, you won't phone him,' he said, pinching the bridge of his nose.

'I can't, Jason.'

He let his hand drop, straightened, and looked across at her.

'Well, I don't see there's much left to say, is there?'

'Please, Jason,' she said, stepping forward. 'We could talk. We could...'

'I should go,' he said, then strode from the kitchen.

She trailed him into the lounge, but stalled by the sofa. 'It doesn't have to be like this,' she said, as he swerved into the hallway. The front door opened, closed. She stood there, motionless. Outside a car door slammed, an engine started, revved, receded. A stillness settled in the house.

*

'Apparently,' Debbie said, 'he's been seeing a woman round the corner and she never knew.' She was talking about her friend, Sheila, who worked in the Co-op. 'I said she could stay with us for a while. Not that Pete's happy about it. But what else was I going to do?' She stood, holding her cup, then extended a hand towards Miriam.

Miriam saved the document, an ENT referral, and passed her cup across.

'She was in bits. Drank two bottles of wine then fell asleep on the sofa.'

'I'm sure she'll get through it,' Miriam said, distantly. She covered her mouth as a yawn overwhelmed her.

'Late night?' Debbie asked, smirking at the end of the desk. 'What you been up to, Miriam?'

Miriam glanced up. 'Trying to do my Spanish.' She didn't

mention that she hadn't looked at it again after Jason left.

'I don't know how you do it.' Debbie moved across the office. 'I don't want to think about anything when I finish here.' The door thumped shut behind her.

Miriam found herself gazing vacantly at the leaning rubber plant in the corner, its glossy green leaves. And she could feel it coming again, the wash of sadness, the aftershock of an old grief. She was tired this morning, felt old. Behind her, the bell on the reception desk rang.

Miriam pushed back her chair, slowly pressed herself to her feet then tugged down the hem of her jacket. She lit a weary smile as she pulled the lever to open the plastic slats.

'Good morning, Miss Bennett,' she said. 'How are you?'

'Oh, you know,' Miss Bennett chuckled, 'soldiering on. What else can you do?'

JOSH

Rain droned on the high metal roof; one of the suspended strip lights was flickering again.

Josh sat at the end of the long steel bench. He was wearing his coat; there was no heating in the warehouse. Hunching forward, he stared at the computer screen, studying the photograph of a pub's dining area. It was a bit shabby, a bit 1980s, but there was definitely potential. And it was cheap. He just needed to raise the money...

A stab of laughter echoed through from the pharmacy side of the building. Josh clicked onto the next image, the pub's kitchen. The kitchen, that's where he belonged, or it had been until five weeks ago when the restaurant's owner gathered the staff for a meeting. 'Look,' he'd said, 'I don't know how to tell you this...' Bankrupt, he'd announced. Josh had loved the restaurant's kitchen, the heat, the smells, the challenge, the satisfaction…

His mobile phone was ringing, vibrating on the bench. He bent forward, checked the incoming number. It was Frank, his uncle. Why hadn't he thought of Frank before? He picked up the phone, thumbed the connection.

'Josh?' Frank sounded flustered.

'Alright, Frank?'

'You free after work?'

'I can be.' There was noise down the line, a muffled friction. 'Frank?'

'How about The Eight Bells?' Frank resumed. 'Half five?'

'Perfect.'

'Customer,' Frank whispered.

Josh listened to the silence. 'Frank?' He stared at the phone's display; the call had ended. Josh smiled slightly. Frank had always been a touch odd; probably the effect of being holed up in his carpet shop for too long.

'You busy then?' someone said.

He skewed round on his seat. It was Beena from the pharmacy. She was standing at the end of the bench, wearing a blue tabard, holding a clipboard to her chest. She was young, had long black hair with a fringe down to her eyebrows.

'Rushed off my feet,' he lied. The last delivery had arrived a couple of hours ago; he'd been idling since. 'What can I get you?'

She laid her clipboard on the bench. 'One Zopiclone,' she

said, tracing under the words with a finger, 'a box of antiseptic swabs and one of sharps. Blues.'

He stood, meandered towards her. 'I'll grab the Zopiclone.' He swung right at the end of the bench, then passed the pallets of unmade boxes he was supposed to construct during the quiet times. Music was leaking through from the pharmacy radio. He pulled open the door into the walk-in fridge and entered.

The chiller unit sluiced a steady breeze across him as he bent to a low shelf and grasped a small glass bottle. He closed the door behind him then hesitated, staring at the bottle in his palm. Five weeks he'd been working here now. Five weeks! Doling out drugs and ointments, sending out medical supplies, taking in deliveries, making boxes. And for £8.21 an hour. It was insulting. He was a trained chef.

He drifted back to the bench, placed the bottle beside the clipboard. As he loafed across to his seat, Beena emerged from the run of stock-stacked shelves. 'How's it all going in there?' he asked, sitting.

'Hectic,' she said, dropping a pile of the boxes onto her clipboard. 'And Lauren won't stop talking about her horse.' She lifted the clipboard, gripped the bottle. 'She's been on about it all day. I mean, why do I care if Tilly's got a cough?'

Josh laughed.

'Now then, young Josh.' Terry the delivery driver appeared from behind Beena. He was short and bald, in his mid-sixties. He moved across, angled his back to the shelves and began rolling up his shirt sleeves, ensuring his tattoos were visible. He'd been in the navy and mentioned it most days.

Josh watched Beena withdraw, then glanced over at the driver. The light from the flickering bulb was playing on his glossy scalp.

'You shouldn't be chatting up the girls…' Terry started.

'I wasn't…'

'You're a married man.'

Josh shook his head.

'And you've a kid on the way.'

Josh turned back to the computer screen, 'So, where've you been today then?'

'Brighton.' Terry stepped toward the bench, leaned back against it, folding his arms, crossing his feet. 'You'll never guess what I saw.'

Josh sensed Terry was about to share one of his stories.

'Right, there were these two fellas…' Terry began.

Josh swivelled round. 'Sorry, Terry,' he cut in, 'could you tell me later?'

Terry straightened, pulled back his shoulders.

'I've just got to concentrate on this.' Josh jerked a thumb at the screen.

'What is it?' Terry pushed up one of his sleeves.

'Just stock-control stuff.' He watched Terry stalk away; heading to pester the women in the pharmacy presumably. Josh turned to the screen again. He was certain he could make this pub work. His phone beeped. He leaned forward, tapped the touchscreen. It was a text from Molly, his girlfriend, reminding him to buy milk on the way home.

The daylight had already drained away. A scouring wind blew, its sharp edge steeled by a fine, icy rain. With his head bowed and his hands sunk deep in his coat pockets, he hurried by the train station, its car park cluttered. He veered onto the main street into town then jogged across the road, picking through a gap in the traffic. He strode past the boarded-up shop, the cinema, the cobbler's. Yes, he would ask Uncle Frank to loan him the money. Why not? Frank could afford it. And he'd always wanted to help, ever since Josh's dad, Frank's brother, had died. Josh had been thirteen then.

He rounded the corner where the butcher's shop had once been. It was a brilliantly lit kebab house now, leaking greasy richness into the brittle evening. At the brow of the brief incline he passed St Lawrence's church, its flint wall corralling a flock of leaning gravestones, its tower rising against the night. The pavement curved around the pub's bellied wall; the light spilling from the sweating windows fell across the slicked flagstones.

He pushed through the age-dark door then paused, waiting as a chocolate-coloured Labrador crossed his path, its choker-chain swinging. Josh glanced around. There were four men clustered near the bar, talking loudly under the low, black-beamed ceiling. To the right, a coal fire glowed in the dusty inglenook. At a table beside it, a grizzled old guy was huddled over a newspaper, his pint to hand. There was no sign of Frank. Josh sidled by the men and leaned an elbow on the bar, watching as the barman pressed a button on the glass-washer. The water jets hissed; the barman turned, florid-faced, moist-eyed.

'What can I get you?' he asked.

Josh ordered a Guinness. He was patting his pockets, searching out some money when the men beside him launched a volley of greetings.

'Now then, Frank,' one of them said.

Josh turned, saw his uncle gently clap one of the men on the shoulder. 'We'll talk later,' he said, nodding towards Josh, detaching from the group. The men rekindled their discussion.

'How long have you been here?' Frank asked.

'Just got here.'

'I'll get these.' Frank leaned over the bar, 'And can I get a Doom Bar as well?'

The barman delivered Josh's Guinness.

'So…' Frank said, unzipping his coat, 'How are you, Josh?'

'I'm all right thanks.'

'It can't be far off now, can it?' Frank briskly rubbed his hands together, blew into them.

'What can't?' Josh looked across, watched the barman heave at the pump, filling Frank's glass.

'Fatherhood.'

Josh smiled ruefully. 'Yeah, a couple of weeks.'

Frank reached inside his jacket, dug out a dog-eared wallet.

He plucked at a note and held it over the bar as the barman delivered the beer.

'How's Molly?' Frank asked.

'OK, I think. A bit stressed,' Josh admitted. 'Could have done without me losing my job.'

'Mmm…' Frank took his change, dropped it into a pocket then lifted his glass. 'Cheers,' he said, winking.

Josh raised his glass, swilled back a mouthful. He could feel the warmth from the fire seeping through the back of his trousers.

Frank sucked the froth from his top lip then cocked his head toward the far side of the room. 'Do you want to sit?' As Frank turned, one of the men touched his arm.

'What do you think we should do, Frank?' the man asked.

Josh waited briefly, then, when he heard one of the men mention the Chambers of Commerce, he steered round the group, left Frank behind. He crossed to the far side of the pub where a few tables were randomly stationed. The table nearest the toilets was silently occupied by an elderly couple, each staring off in different directions.

Josh settled over by the wall, positioned his back to the radiator and looked towards the bar. Yes, he'd ask Frank for the start-up money. To be fully repaid, with interest, of course. Frank could be a silent partner, could even take a share of the profits. He sipped his Guinness. He just had to wait for the right moment.

Frank was walking towards him. He dragged out a chair.

'Sorry about that,' he said, sitting.

'What was it about?' Josh nodded towards the gang of men.

'Oh, business rates.' Frank grimaced, shook his head. 'Killing the place.'

'Ah.' Josh considered Frank's oily black stubble, the looseness of his flesh.

'The florist closed last week. Twenty years she'd been there.' Frank slid a glance towards the old couple. Beyond them, the dog was lapping water from a bowl. 'Anyway,' Frank wafted a hand, sat back, 'that's not why I called, Josh.'

Josh turned his glass by its base.

'Right,' Frank began. 'So, I just wanted to run something past you.' He leaned forward, interlocked his fingers.

Josh laughed softly. 'Yeah, there's something I wanted…'

'So, what are your plans, Josh?'

'In what way?'

'For the future. You know, work-wise. Your mum told me you're temping.'

Josh pulled a face, shrugged.

'You can't do that forever, can you?'

'I'm not planning to do it forever,' Josh snapped. He laid a palm on the table. 'I want to get back into the restaurant business, running my own place…'

'Yeah, but the last place went belly-up, didn't it?' Frank took a drink.

'Restaurants can make good money,' Josh qualified.

'They're risky though, aren't they?'

'Not if you've got the right location, the right menu…'

'And it's the hours, isn't it?'

Josh sensed Frank wasn't listening. 'I actually wanted to talk to you about…' He just needed to steer the conversation.

'You know, things'll change when the baby's born.'

'Yes, I do know that, Frank.' Josh screwed his eyes shut, sighed.

'Look, I'm not meaning to lecture you, Josh.' Frank reached across the table but stopped short of touching Josh's hand. 'There is another option, though.' Frank fixed him with a look.

Josh sipped his drink, met Frank's eye.

'You see, Gill wants me to slow down.' Frank lifted his glass, gestured with it so the liquid swirled. 'Keeps telling me I'm missing the grandkids growing up.' He drank, then placed his glass precisely on the beermat. 'And what it is…' He laid his hands flat on the table. 'I'm getting older, Josh. And Dan and Laura, well, they've got their own lives.'

Josh ran his fingers down the side of his glass. He hardly needed reminding how well Dan and Laura's lives had turned out.

'So, I've talked it over with Gill. And with your mum.'

'Talked what over?' A frown buckled Josh's brow.

'And I'd like to do this for you.'

'What are you talking about, Frank?' Josh smiled indulgently.

'Well…' Frank hung his head, looking at Josh from under his wispy eyebrows. 'Now, don't go off at the deep end…'

he sucked a deep breath. 'But, I'd like you to take over the business.' He raised a hand in pre-emptive defence. 'I'll train you up, let you find your feet. And then it's yours.'

Josh's smile slipped.

'Now, don't make a decision straight away,' Frank counselled. 'Just think about it.'

Josh's gaze slid past Frank's shoulder, settled on the fire.

'Talk it over with Molly. Think it through.' Frank leaned into Josh's sight-line, nodded knowingly. 'It's a good business, Josh.'

'I'll think about it,' he said. He pressed his lips together and slowly nodded. How could he ask Frank for money now?

'Good lad.' Frank squinted appreciatively, then leaned back, his eyes bright with relief. 'I wasn't sure how you'd react.'

'No, I do appreciate it,' Josh said. 'I'm just a bit, you know…'

'I'd like it if I could do something to help you two.'

'Thanks, Frank,' Josh mumbled.

'Look at Gill and me. We wouldn't have been where we are now without help from her dad. We didn't have two pennies. And Daniel was on the way.' Frank took a long drink, gasped as he sat back. 'Anyway. There it is. I've said it.' He tapped the table-top then nodded at Josh's glass. 'Fancy another?' He stood stiffly.

'No, I should go. Molly's expecting me.'

'Same again?' Frank had turned towards the bar before Josh could protest.

Josh stared at the stagnant froth on the sides of his glass.

What had just happened? He looked over at the bar. One of the men had peeled from the group, was talking into Frank's ear.

★

The traffic had dwindled now. Josh veered left at the roundabout by the kebab shop, pulled up his collar. The wind had grown keener, colder, was buffeting at his back.

Carpets? Why would he want to sell carpets? He had bigger dreams than that. A restaurant made perfect sense. But people like Frank had never had any ambitions. They didn't understand. And why wouldn't anyone tell him he should pursue his own ambitions; build his own life? Josh reached into his pocket, pulled out his phone and scrolled down the contacts. He dialled the number.

'Joshua!' the voice said.

'You at home, Rob?' Josh shielded the phone with his free hand, blocking the wind's bluster.

'Just me and the kids.'

'All right if I pop round?'

'As long as you don't mind it being dinner-time.'

Above the wind's rumble Josh heard a child grizzle in the background. 'I'm a minute away.'

'Roger!'

He swerved onto the side street, his thigh brushing the voluminous ivy that erupted over a garden wall. Nursery

Road; it was the sort of leafy street Josh could live on, if he had the money. Spacious, well-kept terraces at the lower end, then more modern houses further along, built incrementally as the town had expanded. Rob lived in the last of the Victorian terraces, just before the kink in the road. He was Josh's oldest friend; they'd been at school together.

Josh knocked hard on the door so that the brass letterbox rattled. There were rapid, clumping footfalls, the door swept back and Rob stood grinning through a neatly trimmed beard, his arms outstretched.

'What do you think?' he asked. He was wearing a tight, white T-shirt with 'FLASH' in red across its front. Rob beckoned him in, then without waiting for a reply, jogged along the hallway. He was wearing shorts, ankle socks, his densely haired legs exposed. The TV was on in the lounge.

'I've always wanted one. Saw it on Ebay,' Rob called.

Josh followed him into the kitchen. A curly-haired toddler was sitting by the table in a high chair. Rob placed his hands on his hips, spread his legs, pushed out his gut. 'You don't think it makes me look like a gay icon, do you?'

'A bit,' Josh admitted.

'That's what Zoe said.'

'Where is she?'

'Pilates. Are you going to eat that, Ryan?' Rob bent to the boy, smiled manically into his face. 'Go on, have a few more spoonfuls.' He straightened. 'Everything all right, Isla?' he called. He waited, his head raised attentively, but no reply came. 'Is your dinner OK, Isla?' he repeated more loudly. A faint 'yes' filtered through from the lounge. 'So, how's things, Josh? How's Molly?' Rob picked a plate from the draining board, began to dry it. 'Any news?'

'Something a bit bizarre's just happened.'

The toddler in the high chair squawked and banged his spoon on the edge of the dish. 'Don't do that, you little shit.' Rob hopped sideways, removing the dish from the child's reach. 'Do you want any more or not?' His son extended a grasping hand. 'This isn't ammunition, you know.' The child laughed, banged the spoon on the tray of the high chair. Rob placed the dish in front of the boy again. 'So what's happened, Josh?'

'I've just seen Frank.'

'Watson's Carpets Frank?'

'Mmm.'

'Did us a fantastic deal on the bedrooms.'

'Did he?' Josh inquired dryly.

'So, what's the problem?' Crockery clattered as Rob slid the plate into a cupboard. The child gurgled.

Josh unbuttoned his coat. 'He's just offered me his business.'

'How do you mean?' Rob craned round the cupboard door.

'Said he wants to retire. Wants me to take it over. I'm still trying to understand it, to be honest.'

Rob stared across at him, open-mouthed, eyes wide. 'That's fantastic.'

'It's carpets, Rob.'

'What's wrong with carpets?' He picked up another plate, wiped it front and back.

'I'm a chef. I should have my own restaurant. That's where I belong.'

'I'd bite his hand off, if I were you.'

'Yeah, well…'

'You could sell carpets. And, you know, being realistic for a second, the restaurant will probably never happen, will it?'

'What does that mean?'

'You know what I mean. Things change when you have children. They just do.'

'Why does everyone keep telling me that?'

'Well, it's true.' Rob slid the plate into the cupboard.

'But there are things I want to do.' Josh scanned the chaotic worktop, then looked down at a plastic fire engine beside his foot, nudged it with his shoe.

'It's the same for everyone. But they make it…' The child was beating its dish again. As Rob stepped forward to intervene the dish flipped over. Josh watched Rob glance down at the orange daub across his T-shirt, saw his brief horror soften to a grin. 'So you don't like the T-shirt, Ryan?' Rob said, righting the dish. 'Have you told Molly?'

'No. Not yet.'

'Just give me a minute, Josh.' Rob skipped across to the sink, gathered a cloth. 'You've got it fekkin' everywhere, Ryan,' he said, dropping to his knees.

Josh wandered through to the lounge. Isla, Rob's five-year-old, was standing in front of the sofa, transfixed by the television. *Lady and the Tramp* was on. She was gripping an intact slice of pizza; there was a full plate on the sofa behind her.

'Hello Isla.' Josh sat on the arm of a chair. 'What are you watching?'

Isla turned her large dark eyes towards him then looked back at the TV.

'How's the dancing going?'

'OK,' she said. She nibbled the tip off her pizza.

Rob trotted into the room then halted, blocking Josh's view of the television. 'Haven't you eaten that yet, Isla?'

She stared at the screen, chewing slowly.

'Come on, eat up before it's cold. You've got to take Frank up on this, Josh.'

Josh stared at the damp patch on Rob's shirt where a cloth had been applied; the stain remained, smudged but vivid still. He followed Rob back into the kitchen.

'You'll be set for life.' Rob lifted the child from its chair, began bouncing the boy on his hip. 'You'll be able to buy a house in a couple of years.'

'But I couldn't give a shit about carpets.'

*

Josh ambled up the middle of Nursery Road, passing the

newer houses, treading the white line. The top of the road ran into a more recent estate, the houses of different design, built with a sandier brick. He followed the long curve until the road terminated at the junction. Beyond the ragged hedge opposite, the gym, Finesse, seeped light and noise. Beside it, the playing fields rolled out into a silent, black expanse. What would his dad have said? Probably something about responsibility, security and how children change things, just like everyone else. He was sick of hearing it.

He turned left, walked past St Hilda's, the private school, its red-brick buildings half-screened behind a mesh of bare branches. The rain had washed mud down from the new development at the top of the road where diggers had been preparing the ground; the gutters were silted with alluvial deposits. But why did he have to give up on the restaurant? He walked on past the mini-market then cornered into his street. Occasionally, between the primly tended lawns, there were overrun gardens littered with abandoned fridges and fox-gnawed bin liners. And anyway, what was so good about carpets?

*

He pressed the front door closed behind him. Unbuttoning his coat, he eased into the lounge. Pictures flickered silently on the TV screen, the sound muted. Molly was on the sofa, her feet up. She was huge now, domed, only three weeks from her due date. He threw his coat onto the armchair.

'Where've you been?' Molly asked, shifting uncomfortably.

'Frank wanted to see me.'

'What about?'

Josh walked across the room, sat on the edge of the sofa beside her outstretched legs. He hitched round to face her. 'How was your day?'

'OK. A couple of the girls from the salon called round.' She'd finished work at the hairdresser's a month ago.

He reached across and rested a hand on her bump. She laid her hand on his.

'So what did Frank want?'

'Oh, I just think he wanted to talk about fatherhood. You know, one of his instructive little chats.' He glanced at her, noticed she was eyeing him.

'Have you been drinking?'

'I only had a couple. Frank insisted.'

'Did you forget the milk?'

He squeezed his eyes shut. 'Shit. Sorry.' He looked at her. 'Do we need it tonight?'

'We'll survive, I suppose.'

'I'll go in the morning.' He turned over his hand, interlocked his fingers with hers. 'What do you want for dinner?' She raised her shoulders, pouted slightly. 'I could cook something if you want. A feast.' But somehow he didn't feel like cooking. 'Or...' he paused thoughtfully, '...or we could just get a pizza.'

'We can't afford that.'

'Let's just pretend we can. What would you like?'

'We can't afford it, Josh.'

'Just say we can. What would you like?'

'Ham and pineapple?' She laughed slightly.

'Right, that's decided then.' He slapped his thighs, stood, rounded the sofa and walked through to the kitchen. He switched on the light then pulled open the drawer where they stuffed the takeaway menus along with the other odds and ends that had no particular home: a twist of string, a Pritt Stick, random batteries, a torch.

'How was work?' Molly called.

He drifted back into the lounge. 'Oh, the usual awfulness, you know.' He stepped across to the armchair, pulled his phone from a coat pocket, then sat down on the sofa again. 'I saw the perfect pub today,' he said, thumbing in the number. 'It'd make a fantastic restaurant.'

'We've been through this,' Molly said softly.

'I know.'

'So what did Frank really want?'

He looked at her from the corner of his eye. 'I think he was trying to sell me something.' He dialled the number, held the phone to his ear. 'Ham and pineapple?' he checked.

'And can you get some ice cream? I mean, if we're celebrating.'

'I wouldn't call it celebrating, exactly.' He said it sideways. The pizza man answered, Josh placed his order, rang off. 'Forty minutes,' he said, dropping the phone onto the floor.

'And did Frank say anything else?'

Josh stared at the television, the silent images shifting. 'Just that he wanted to slow down.' He picked the remote control from where it nestled against Molly's thigh. 'Anything good on tonight?' He flicked through the channels, pulled up the guide.

'Your mum called me today.'

'Ah.' Josh nodded, smiled resignedly, placed the remote control on the arm of the sofa.

'She told me.'

'Told you what?'

'Frank's business.'

He shifted, stared at her stomach, then gently stroked it.

'When were you going to tell me?' she asked, softly.

Josh shrugged. He lifted up her T-shirt and laid his palm onto her swollen belly, left it there.

'You have accepted it, haven't you?'

He shook his head.

'Ring him then. Tell him.'

'Tell him what?'

'That you want to do it.'

'Later,' he said, absently.

'When, Josh?'

He could feel movement under his hand, sudden and definite. The baby was kicking.

SHEILA

The December afternoon had closed in. It was dark already.

As she trailed him up the short path, she glanced at the miniature Christmas tree glittering in the bay window. Darren reached out, pressed the doorbell.

'It's a very desirable area, this,' he said over his shoulder. 'Don't stay on the market long.'

Sheila buried her chin into the collar of her coat, the moist warmth of her breath reflecting back onto the lower half of her face. A terraced house. At this point in her life. The door opened but she couldn't see round Darren's pin-striped back.

'Hello, Miss Bennett. We're here for the 4.30 viewing.' Darren spoke loudly, slowly.

Miss Bennett was lingering in the hallway. She was white-haired, had bright, eager eyes; was wearing a cardigan, slacks.

Sheila nodded a greeting as she tracked Darren through to the lounge.

'With a place like this you've got to look at the potential...' Darren began, but Sheila wasn't listening. The carpet was a faded pink; the sofa, dated but not worn; there was an armchair backed up under the window; a small, central coffee table; a TV in the corner. The room wasn't a bad size.

'...It'd be easy to stamp your own identity...'

Sheila followed Darren through the lounge, past the stairs.

'...only minor cosmetic...'

She looked round the dining room: a small, oak table and four chairs, a floral print hanging on the wall. Darren flicked a switch. Through the patio doors she could see a brief lawn leading down to a rickety shed. Somewhere she could potter. She scanned the compact kitchen. The place was better than she'd thought it would be.

For a moment, Sheila paused in the dining room doorway, watching Miss Bennett pull closed the curtains in the lounge, then she followed Darren up the stairs.

The bathroom was functional. She'd prefer a shower, but that could be remedied. The master bedroom was a reasonable size; there was even a built-in wardrobe. In the spare room there was plenty of space for storage.

'...only cosmetic...' Darren repeated as he led back downstairs. '...at a very accessible price.' He paused in the lounge, looking back over Sheila's head. 'Thank you, Miss Bennett,' he called sonorously.

Miss Bennett trotted through from the kitchen.

'Was everything all right?' she asked, breathless.

'It's a lovely home,' Sheila mumbled, her words muffling in the collar of her coat.

'Everything was fine, thank you.' Darren said, continuing through the lounge. 'Thanks again, Miss Bennett,' he called, wrenching open the front door.

In the hallway, Sheila hesitated, the cold air washing over her as she watched Darren saunter splay-footed up the path. He stopped beside his car, jabbing at his smartphone. There was a gentle tug at Sheila's coat-sleeve. She looked round, down into Miss Bennett's upturned face.

'You like it, don't you?' the old lady asserted, quietly, confidentially.

Sheila drew back her head slightly.

'Why don't you come back and have a proper look round,' Miss Bennett urged.

Sheila hunched her shoulders, frowned. 'I could, I suppose,' she murmured, uncertain.

'Tomorrow?' Miss Bennett gripped Sheila's forearm lightly.

Sheila nodded towards the estate agent. 'I'll organise it with Darren.'

'Oh, don't bother with him. Shall we say five?'

Stepping out into the premature evening, Sheila pushed her hands deep into her pockets.

'Tomorrow at five, then,' Miss Bennett said. She gave a little wave, then closed the door.

Sheila moved along the corridor to the door of her flat, unlocked it. She palmed on the light-switch. Looking blankly at the still-sealed boxes stacked against the walls, she slid the keys back into her coat pocket. For a few seconds she listened to the stark, lifeless silence, then, crossed to the television, turned it on. The on-screen voices babbled their quiz show bonhomie as she walked through to the kitchen.

She stared into the fridge, empty save for a half-full carton of milk and a tub of margarine. Yanking open the freezer, she dragged out the top drawer and extracted a solid sachet of cod in butter sauce, then slid it skating across the worktop towards the hob. As she kneed the door shut, the gas boiler on the wall flared into life, emitting sharp, metallic cracks. Turning to pick a pan from the draining board, she heard the first soft ripple of rain against the window over the sink, glanced up. A ghostly pale, translucent face stared back at her; for a split-second she didn't recognise herself. She touched a hand to her cheek. How old she looked. Too old to be starting again.

She forked in a mouthful of rice, her eyes fixed on the screen, the images of broken and bloodied streets. Bombs were being dropped on some faraway country. Resting her fork on her plate, she reached down the side of the armchair, groped for the remote control. She changed the channel, found the local news. Better stories about potholes and parking charges than death and suffering. Especially when she was eating. Her mobile phone was ringing.

Sighing, she stood, placed her plate on the seat of the armchair and crossed to the door where her coat hung from a hook. She pulled the phone from her pocket, sighed again.

'Hello, Mum.'

'Sheila?'

'What's wrong?' Sheila watched the images on the screen; a man in an anorak standing by a swollen river.

'Nothing's wrong. I'm just seeing how you are.'

'Everything's fine, Mum,' Sheila said wearily.

'What are you doing? What's that in the background?' There was a note of suspicion in her mother's voice.

'It's the television. I'm trying to eat my dinner,' Sheila explained, patiently.

'Not those cod things again.'

Sheila rolled her eyes, stared up at the Artexed ceiling.

'You should be looking after yourself.'

'I am looking after myself.'

'And you shouldn't be sitting on your own watching television. You should be getting out there, meeting people, not moping, feeling sorry for yourself.'

Sheila watched the pictures of a court-house. Someone on trial for something.

'Are you there, Sheila?'

'I went to see a house today,' she said, flatly.

'Where?'

'Borovere Avenue.'

'Where's that?'

'Bottom end of town.'

'I still don't understand why you'd want to stay there after everything.'

'You're always telling me I should be moving on. That's what I'm doing,' Sheila said, exasperated.

'But if you moved somewhere else you'd get more for your money. You'd be better off. You could move back up here.'

Sheila was shaking her head. 'I'll make my own decisions, Mum.'

'I only worry about you, Sheila.'

'I know you do. Look, I've got to go, my food's going cold. I'll call you later.' She knew she wouldn't. 'OK. Bye.'

★

After the early rush of workers and school kids, the tide of customers in the mini-market had slowed to a steady flow. Sheila stood behind the counter, her arms folded. She glanced up at the clock over the shuttered cigarettes. Three hours until Ken started his shift and took over on the till. Then she could escape and re-fill the shelves until it was time to finish.

She looked along the bread aisle. Helen, the overweight store-manager, was straddling wide as she bent to a low shelf, assessing stock, a broad crescent of moon-white flesh exposed where her jacket and shirt had ridden up.

'You're late.' That's how Helen had started this morning.

'No, I'm not.' Sheila had nodded towards the clock.

'And where's your hat?'

'Hat?' Sheila had said, feigning innocence.

'Your Santa hat, Sheila.'

'I'm not wearing one,' she'd said defiantly.

Helen had snorted knowingly. 'Well, we'll see what the area manager has to say about that.'

Sheila watched Helen straighten and pull down her jacket, hitch up her trousers, then wander round the top of the aisle. There was no way she would be wearing a Santa hat; it wasn't in her job description.

The automatic doors swooshed open, admitting two builders, both wearing high-vis jackets and mud-caked rigger boots. They were working on a development at the top end of town, came in every day. Their voices rose from beyond the shelves; Helen's braying laughter split the air.

Sheila turned as the entrance doors swooshed again. A young woman entered with a wailing new-born in a pram, a wide-eyed toddler bouncing along beside her. Sheila felt the sudden deep ache, the cavernous sadness opening in her chest, swallowing her from the inside. Malcolm had never wanted children. 'I can't commit to that sort of responsibility,' he used to say. And she'd accepted it. Then one day, it had been too late.

Helen was laughing again.

'Come in, luvvie,' Miss Bennett said, backing into the house.

Sheila mustered a timid half-smile as she stepped through to the lounge. Lingering by the coffee table, she could hear a low rumble, the kettle boiling in the kitchen.

Miss Bennett shuttled through towards the dining room. 'Tea?' she asked without looking back.

'Erm, yes. Thank you.' Sheila watched the woman veer from view.

'Milk and sugar?' called the voice from the kitchen.

'Just milk, please, Miss Bennett.'

'Irene,' the woman corrected, a teaspoon clinking in a cup.

Sheila unbuttoned her navy pea-coat. There weren't any photographs, she noted, though there were six or seven Christmas cards on the sill in the bay window. On the drawers by the sofa, a carriage clock ticked softly. She noticed a tall, pine bookcase behind the door from the hallway, leaned towards it, scanning the contents: Maeve Binchy, Marian Keyes, antique editions of Dickens. On the shelves below, *The Rudiments of Music*, musical scores, books on composition, music theory. She straightened when Irene shuffled back into the lounge, transporting two mugs on a tray.

Sheila perched on the edge of the sofa, her elbows on her knees, cradling the cup in both hands, warming her chilled fingers. Irene carefully shunted herself back into her chair until her slippered feet didn't quite touch the ground. She patted her hair, then smiled at Sheila.

'It's very kind of you inviting me back like this,' Sheila said.

'It's a pleasure.' Irene settled her elbows on the armrests, nestled the cup in her lap. 'So you like the house then?' Irene smiled again

'Yes, it's very nice.' Sheila nodded, sipped her tea. 'How long have you been here?'

'It's been perfect for me.'

'Mmm…' Sheila nodded cautiously, trying to discern a hearing aid.

'But it's getting too much now. The stairs you see.'

'You still seem very active.' Sheila sipped her tea again.

Irene laughed slightly. 'It's more difficult when you're on your own, though.'

Sheila nodded. Listening to the insistent tick of the clock, she studied the tannin ring on the inside of her mug.

'Are you on your own?' Irene asked.

For a moment, Sheila's face clouded.

'Yes,' she whispered, turning the cup so her fingers passed through the handle.

'What happened, dear?' Irene leaned forward.

For an instant, Sheila stared searchingly at Irene, then she bowed her head.

'Divorced.' Sheila pressed her lips together, squinted. When she looked up, Irene was watching her, waiting. She was nodding encouragement, smiling. 'It just happened, really.'

'That's how life is,' Irene said, gently.

'It started in January…' Sheila sniffed. 'He started dressing differently…different haircut.' She spoke quickly, towards the coffee table. She didn't know why, but she couldn't stop the words from flooding out. 'Then, in February, he started taking the dog out for these long walks. At night. Three hours sometimes. Was only getting in at two in the morning.' Sheila looked up at Irene. 'I asked him, you know, "What's going on?" but he just said that he enjoyed the night air. Then the dog got fleas. So I asked him, "Where's the dog got fleas from?" And he just said, "Sniffing hedgehogs."' Sheila dipped her chin, widened her eyes.

Irene laughed quietly.

'And like an idiot, I trusted him… I always trusted him.'

'That's only natural, dear.'

'Mmm…' Sheila pouted sourly, arched her eyebrows. 'Anyway, not long after, I couldn't find my mobile. Needed to make a call, you see.' She cocked her head to one side, stared past Irene, at the miniature Christmas tree, trying to remember what that call was, but the detail eluded her. She shook her head. 'So I got his mobile out of his coat. Noticed there was an answer phone message. I know I shouldn't have done, but I listened to it. Someone playing love songs down the phone. Katie bloody Melua! Sorry.'

Irene's gaze didn't waver.

'I didn't say anything, not straight away. But I followed him when he took the dog out. He let himself into a house just round the corner. Two hundred yards away. Had his own key.' Sheila straightened her back for an instant, then hunched forward again. 'A cat came scooting out when he went in. And suddenly it all made sense.'

'Mmm…' said Irene.

'He denied it at first. Lied through his teeth. But I knew what I'd seen.'

Irene nodded again.

'In the end he said, "Sheila, it is possible for a man to love two women." Said he couldn't make a choice, so I made it for him. And here we are.' Sheila turned a palm upwards. 'I mean, it'd been going on for months and no one told me.'

'It must have been very difficult.'

Sheila reached into her pocket, pulled out a tissue, blew her nose, then pushed the tissue up her sleeve.

'Sounds almost comical when I say it.' Sheila sighed, sipped her tea. 'Seventeen years like it never happened. He's living with her now.' She dipped her chin, a mischievous glint in her eyes. 'Good luck to him, I say. She's got a beard. I mean, a proper beard.'

As Irene laughed, Sheila felt herself blush, certain she'd revealed too much. She lowered her gaze, swilled back the rest of her tea.

'Thanks,' she said, raising the cup. She looked away again, unwilling to meet the woman's eye, guilty, like a child who's accidentally disclosed an incriminating secret.

'Would you like to look round again?'

'Is that all right?' Sheila felt the relief wash through her.

'Of course it is. Help yourself.'

Sheila stood, held out her cup. 'Where do you want this?'

'Just pop it in the kitchen, if you don't mind.' Irene leaned back.

★

Sheila descended the stairs slowly, thoughtful, then stepped back into the lounge.

Irene was manoeuvring to the edge of her chair. 'Everything all right?' she asked, struggling crookedly to her feet.

'It's a lovely home.' Sheila began to button up her coat.

Irene exhaled heavily. 'Yes, it'll be difficult to leave.' She wrinkled her nose.

'Where will you go?' Sheila said, turning up her collar.

Irene seemed not to hear, was looking towards the dining room, distracted. For a moment, the two women stood in silence.

'Well,' Sheila said, bending her knees. 'I'd better be off.' She sidestepped towards the door, paused. 'Thanks for the tea, Irene. And thanks for letting me look round again. It was really helpful.'

Irene shuffled towards Sheila and laid an arthritic hand on her sleeve. 'I think you'll like living here.' Irene's face crumpled into a smile; she blinked, bobbed her head forward and gently squeezed Sheila's arm.

'Thank you,' she murmured, frowning.

'You must come again,' Irene said brightly as she reached across Sheila and pulled the front door open, the cool air rushing in. 'Tomorrow night?'

'I don't think I really need to.' Sheila stepped outside.

'It's better to be sure though, isn't it?' Irene urged.

Sheila shrugged slightly, nodded.

'Shall we say five?' Irene said through a narrowing crack in the door.

Sheila moved off down the hill towards town. It struck her after she crossed the entrance to a Retirement Home. Her stride slowed, she clamped her eyes shut momentarily. 'Oh God!' she whispered. Why had she just blurted all that out to Irene? What would she think of her? She felt rain on her face and watched the rush-hour traffic flitting, flashing past the end of the road. Burying her chin in the collar of her coat, she accelerated.

As usual, Ken had taken over on the counter at two. After a couple of minutes of compulsory conversation, Sheila had drifted away.

She picked a pair of sliced white loaves from the tray of bread, then bent and placed them on the shelf. As she straightened, she swatted at the swinging bobble of her Santa hat so that it flipped back over her head and brushed lightly against her neck. She pressed another pair of loaves together and lifted them to the shelf. The hat, she considered, was just another in a long line of concessions; concessions that had been forced on her. She was sure Helen had enjoyed it.

'I'm afraid the word's come through,' she'd said.

Sheila hadn't responded; she'd been handing a customer

her change at the time.

'The area manager's confirmed that everyone's got to wear a Santa hat. I'm sorry, Sheila, but it'll be a disciplinary matter if you don't.'

'I strongly object on the grounds that this infringes my fundamental human rights.' That's what she should have said. Instead she'd just replied, 'Why aren't you wearing one then?' She'd known it sounded petty as soon as she'd said it.

Sheila collected another couple of sliced whites, placed them on the shelf, patting the last in line to close the gaps. She turned, lifted the empty tray from the stack, paused. Was that it? Life? A Santa hat you're forced to wear? A series of concessions, compromises and failures? She dropped the tray onto the tiled floor; it landed with a clatter.

She'd been betrayed by her husband; wasted her best years. She'd left her home; then there was her mum; and now this Santa hat. No, she'd made the last of her concessions. She was going to buy this house; didn't care what anyone else thought. It was something no one could take away. A little piece of Sheila. A planted flag. It might not be the right thing to do, but she was going to do it anyway.

She pincered a pair of seeded granary loaves, and shoved them roughly onto the next shelf along.

'Would you like a biscuit?' Irene called from the kitchen.

'No, I'm fine, thanks, Irene.'

Sheila pulled off her coat, dropped it over the arm of the

sofa.

'Feel free to look around,' Irene piped.

As Sheila climbed the stairs, she already knew. There was a tranquillity to the house. A calm. It was snug, safe; it didn't have the same drab, oppressive silence as her flat; this was peaceful somehow. She opened the door to the master bedroom. Yes, it was a place where she could begin again. It could be home. A lick of paint, a new carpet. Nothing really. She would put in an offer. Then everyone would know she was moving on.

Back in the lounge, the mugs were already on the coffee table.

'Here you are, luvvie.' Irene came through from the kitchen, holding out the plate so Sheila couldn't refuse.

Sheila placed the plate on the table. Rich Tea. Out of courtesy she picked one up, nibbled off an edge. She glanced at her cup, but wasn't sure she and Irene had reached a sufficient intimacy for her to start dunking biscuits. But more importantly, she needed to discuss money.

'So, do you work?' Irene asked.

Irene leaned forward, reaching for her mug.

'Just at the shop in the middle of town. The Co-op.' Sheila covered her mouth with her hand.

'Oh, I know the one.' Irene was hitching back into her chair.

'It's nothing much. But it keeps me going.' Sheila remembered the previous evening, her confession. 'So what about you?' Questions and feigning an interest, she knew, were the best defence against those difficult personal topics.

Irene sipped her tea, looking over the rim of her cup.

'What did you do?' Sheila nibbled at the biscuit.

'I was a music teacher. Cello.' Irene smiled. 'So lovely hearing the young ones develop. I taught in schools for the last twenty years.'

Sheila widened her eyes appreciatively as she washed the biscuit down with a gulp of tea.

'And you never married.'

Irene's head sank. 'Well, no,' she said towards her lap, 'There was a first violin. In an orchestra. Not a soloist...' Irene's eyes glazed for an instant. 'Quite brilliant, but...'

How long, Sheila wondered, should she wait before she talked about money. She glanced around the room as Irene continued. If she could get the place for £10,000 less than the asking price, with the money from the divorce, the house sale, she would only need a £30,000 mortgage. She could manage that with the job at the shop.

'...that's men though, isn't it? They lie.' Irene pulled her cardigan across her chest.

Yes, she would definitely put in an offer. She'd do it in the morning. She pushed the rest of the biscuit into her mouth, was chewing when she realised Irene had lapsed into silence. She swallowed.

'I was actually thinking of putting in an offer tomorrow,' she said tentatively.

Irene looked up.

'But I just wanted to run it past you first.'

Irene blinked at her.

'How would you feel if I put in an offer of two-eighty. I can afford that. It'll be tight. But I can do it.'

Irene breathed in deeply.

'Would you be happy with that?' Sheila asked.

'I'm sure that'll be fine, luvvie, since it's you...'

Sheila smiled as she reached for another biscuit.

*

Sheila stood behind the counter, absently chewing at a fingernail. It was two o'clock and the estate agent still hadn't called. She'd put the offer in at nine. She pulled her phone from her pocket. Still nothing.

Ken slouched towards the counter, thumbed the code into the keypad and pushed through the security door.

'Hello, Sheila? How's everything?' he said, sidling behind her.

He was fifty-five, had lank, grey hair, with a bald spot hidden under his Santa hat. He'd lived in a caravan since his mum died five years ago. Sheila wasn't in the mood for Ken.

'Not too bad,' she said, edging towards the door. 'You?'

'Oh, you know. Not only is the skylight in the caravan still leaking, but this morning I had a terrible shock...'

She sensed he was about to launch into one of his stories. There was always something with Ken. She shouldered out through the door.

'Sorry,' she said, looking back, 'I've really got to get on. Helen's been at me,' she lied. 'Sorry, Ken.'

The door thumped shut behind her.

'Not a problem,' Ken said, sympathetically.

At four o'clock, the tinned tomatoes fully replenished, Sheila wandered through to the locker room at the back of the shop, pulled off her Santa hat, collected her coat and bag. Why hadn't the estate agents called? It was a certainty; it had been agreed.

She walked back into the shop.

'Night, Sheila,' said Will. He was one of the young ones, in for the evening shift, wearing a pair of flashing reindeer antlers.

'Night, Will.' She turned up her collar as she strode along the aisle towards the entrance. Helen was by the vegetables, leaning on a shopping trolley, talking to a customer.

'...she'd been drinking in the mornings, so they had to sack her...'

Sheila hurried past them. More gossip; about the postwoman this time.

As she approached the automatic doors, she could hear Ken in conference at the counter.

'...right there under the caravan,' he said.

'No. Not in Britain,' a voice counselled.

'Honestly. It was a snake. Massive. Looked like it was smiling at me.'

She didn't stop to find out what he was talking about.

Outside, the darkness was already well settled. The air was sharp, refreshing. It cut away the dull, torpid atmosphere of the shop. She pulled out her mobile phone. Still no reply from the estate agent.

★

She dropped the sachet of cod in butter sauce into the pan of boiling water, then checked the rice simmering beside it. Her head jerked to the right. Was that her phone ringing? She scurried through to the lounge, plunged her hand into her coat. Expectantly, she checked the screen, then tutted and dropped the phone back into her pocket. She couldn't deal with her mum right now.

By ten o'clock the next morning, Sheila could wait no longer. Still she'd heard nothing from the estate agent. While the shop was empty, except for Helen, who was talking to the builders, Sheila crept into the small office behind the counter, pulled out her mobile phone. She dialled the estate agent's number, then flipped the bobble back over her head and lifted the phone to her ear. She held the door ajar with her foot, watching the till.

Darren answered. After the formal niceties Sheila quietly enquired, 'I was just wondering where we are with the house. Have you heard anything back from Irene?'

'Which house was that, Mrs Lomax?'

Sheila's eyes bulged slightly, she sniffed. 'Borovere Avenue.' She could hear Helen cackling out in the shop.

'No, I'm afraid we're still waiting.' Darren sounded reserved, distant.

'Couldn't you give her a nudge, or something?' Sheila pinched the bridge of her nose, squeezed her eyes closed. She hadn't slept last night.

'I can, if that's what you want me to do.'

'If you would.'

'I'll do it now.'

'Thanks. Bye.' She ended the call, dropped the phone into her pocket and edged back out behind the counter. She turned as the doors swooshed open; old George bundled in, broad-hipped, short-legged.

Helen was still talking, laughing in that whinnying way.

'Hello, dear,' said George as he tilted toward the counter holding out his newspaper. He was wearing a paisley cravat.

'Morning, George.'

'How are you today?'

She slid the newspaper past the barcode scanner. 'Not too bad, thanks.'

'Are you ready for Christmas?'

Sheila paused for a second. She hadn't even thought about Christmas.

'Yes, just about,' she deflected. 'How about you?'

'Oh, I'm going to my daughter's. She's looking after me.'

Sheila watched his eyes moisten behind his glasses and remembered that his wife had died earlier in the year. He'd let himself go for a while.

'Well, I hope you have a lovely day,' Sheila said softly.

George smiled weakly.

'That's seventy pence please.'

'Just hang on, I've got it here somewhere.' He fished in his little leather purse.

As George departed, she felt the telephone vibrate in her pocket. She retreated to the side office, answered it.

'Hello?' she said quietly.

It was Darren.

'So what's happening, Darren?'

'Erm...'

Sheila felt her stomach drop.

'Well, I'm not sure how to tell you this...'

'Tell me what, Darren?' There was a quaver in Sheila's voice.

'Erm, well...Miss Bennett has decided to take her house off the market.'

'Taken it off the market?'

'Mmm...'

'Can she do that?'

'If she wants to.'

'But we'd agreed.'

Sheila heard the builders approaching the counter, chatting gruffly between themselves, laughing. She peeked through the crack in the door, saw they were waiting, then let the door close so she was hidden.

'It seems,' said Darren, 'that this isn't the first time she's done it.'

She was shaking her head involuntarily. 'Done what?'

'I was talking to one of my colleagues, and he said they'd had dealings with Miss Bennett before. She's quite well-known for it.'

Sheila stared at the wall numbly; her thoughts had fallen away.

'She's done it a few times apparently.'

'SHOP!' It was one of the builders. They were chuntering between themselves.

'Done what?' Sheila whispered.

'Did she invite you round?'

'I've been back twice. The last two nights. We agreed a price.'

'Shop!' The builder shouted again. Sheila could hear Helen's voice. The door to the counter clunked shut.

'It just seems to be something Miss Bennett does.'

'What are you talking about?'

'She invites people round, to view again, more informally. In the past, apparently, she's had people round for a meal. Had them measuring up for curtains. And then when they put in an offer she takes it off the market.'

'Why?' Sheila asked faintly.

'We think she's just lonely.'

'Lonely?' Sheila shouted. The anger surged. She held the

phone away from her ear, stared at it for a second, then ended the call. She couldn't deal with this. She could hear Helen laughing as the builders' voices receded.

Sheila felt the urge to scream. She pulled off her Santa hat, hurled it at the wall, watching as it silently struck the painted breeze-blocks and flopped onto the floor. She turned savagely when Helen pulled open the door.

'What are you doing, Sheila?' Helen was still smiling.

'I had to take a call.'

'You know you can't leave your till unattended when there are customers in the shop.'

Sheila shrugged.

'Where's your hat?'

Sheila nodded at the hat on the floor.

Calmly, Helen asked, 'Are you going to put that back on?'

Sheila laughed. 'No. I won't be wearing it any more.'

'You're not wearing it?' Helen sounded uncertain.

'Nope.' Sheila unzipped her work fleece.

'This is a disciplinary issue, Sheila. You deserted your post.'

Sheila shrugged again, peeled off her fleece and threw it over the chair by the desk. 'I quit,' she said.

'Don't be like that, Sheila. If you just take your verbal warning everything can go back to normal.'

'Normal?' She raised her voice, fixed Helen with a stare. The manager stepped aside, allowing Sheila to pass.

'What's wrong with you?' she called, as Sheila made her way through the shop to the locker room.

When Sheila reappeared, Helen was waiting, flushed, her hands on her hips.

'You can't just walk out,' she said.

'Watch me,' Sheila muttered, without looking at her. She should have done this months ago.

'What's brought this on?'

Sheila didn't answer, she just walked away. The doors swept open and then she was outside, free. Yes, she would take some time, make some choices, some changes. And Spain, she'd heard, was nice at this time of year.

SEAN

That's what it was. He was being forced to straddle the rift between Rachel and his family.

He was sitting at a desk over by the whitewashed wall, was staring at the floor. Across the room, someone coughed. He glanced up. There were seven in the class today, their easels arranged in a loose semi-circle around the fruit-filled bowl he'd positioned on the central plinth. He looked back at the floor and thought about last night again.

He'd returned late from the studio, had just started to cook. Recently, he'd discovered the joy of soup; he even enjoyed the preparation. He'd heard the front door close. Rachel had been helping with the drama club at the girls' school where she taught. She was walking through the lounge when his phone began to ring. It was his mum. He'd considered dismissing the call, but after the Christmas situation he hadn't felt he could.

'What are you doing on Saturday, Sean?' She hadn't bothered with pleasantries, hadn't asked how he was.

'Why?'

'Michael and Joanne are coming over.'

He'd stirred the sweating vegetables. There was movement behind him, the fridge door opened then closed.

'He'd like us all to be here,' his mum said.

'I don't think I can.' He'd turned, leaned back against the worktop. At the kitchen table, Rachel was pouring a glass of wine. He lifted the phone from his ear, mouthed the word 'Mum' and pulled a face.

'You will come, won't you, Sean?'

'Do I have to?'

'What about Rachel…' his mum began.

'I think she's working on Saturday,' he cut in.

Rachel had shaken her head, held up a hand.

'But you'll definitely be here,' his mother said. 'Ten o'clock.'

'Yes, fine. I'll be there,' he'd said. 'Look, I've got to go.' He'd rung off.

'Why do you never say no to them?' Rachel had asked.

Someone shifted suddenly, a stool-leg squealing across the floor. He looked up. Two of the class, Lydia and Miriam, were whispering between their easels. He stood and sauntered towards to them.

'I thought there might be more men here…' Lydia said. She threw Sean a twinkling smile as he approached.

'So, how are we getting on over here?' He walked round behind Lydia. Folding his arms, he scrutinised the sketch over her shoulder.

'I think it's shaping up nicely,' she said.

'It's looking good,' he encouraged. 'Don't spend too long sketching though.' He moved to her other shoulder. 'This is about bringing out the form with the paint.'

'It's the perfectionist in me.' She chuckled, glancing back at him.

He suspected she was about to tell him she was a glass artist. She told him every week. 'Remember, coarse detail to fine detail. Gradually build it up,' he said, inching away. At the next easel Miriam was swiping lavishly at the canvas with a broad brush.

★

After the class, he drove back out of town. He lived in Benstead, a village three miles beyond Sudleigh's fringes. He sailed through the village centre, passed the short run of set-back shops, the petrol station, the Gospel Hall, and headed down the hill. Slowing as the housing thinned again, he hooked a tight left. Beyond the new estate, the lane ran out into the country, the frost-bitten fields unfurling behind the high hedgerows. He took the next turning, briefly dawdled along a narrower lane then swung in through two tall gateposts. He jolted across the rutted car park towards a cluster of clapboard buildings. He'd rented the smallest of them, was using it as a studio.

Clamping his satchel under his arm, he skipped across the corner of a vast iced-over puddle. The cold hadn't relented all day. He looked across at the next-door unit. The lights were on inside but he could discern no sign of life. It was an antique shop, though he'd never seen any customers visit. Suddenly, he halted, bowed his head then began patting at his pockets. Where had he put the keys?

Inside the studio he flicked the switch by the door; the skylights didn't provide enough light to paint by at this time of year. As the long fluorescent bulbs spluttered into life, he walked towards the easel over by the window. Two years he'd been back in Sudleigh now. He'd lived in London after his training, had thought that's where he should be, where it was at. He'd ended up teaching in prisons, in colleges, working to stay afloat rather than to paint. After eight years, he'd decided to move back to Sudleigh, to start again. He'd begun running a few classes at the Community Centre, doing a bit of private tuition. Then he met Rachel at a party and the relationship had just developed. They'd been living together for nearly eighteen months. And now he'd secured his first proper exhibition. 'The Sudleigh Scene,' he was calling it.

He peeled the dust cover back from the canvas then retreated a step, eyeing the sketched outlines. It was going to be a high-street portrait, three men outside a pub. He wanted to capture the daytime drinkers standing on the pavement, looking out at the viewer with their dead-eyed, hang-dog pride.

He ambled across and dropped his keys onto the long wooden bench against the wall. At the far end of the bench chaos reigned. There were clean brushes standing bristle up in jars; other brushes were plunged head-first into turps or water; there were tubes of paint, pans of watercolours, palettes, stubs of charcoal, scattered rags, a kettle. At this end he maintained a clear stretch. He laid down his satchel, unfastened the clasps and drew out his laptop. There was a picture of the men he wanted to portray saved somewhere. He'd caught them with his camera on a recent sortie into town. But he needed to look at it again, to study the characters.

He flipped up the screen and typed in the password. As he waited he gazed out of the window. Across the fields, a thin band of copper cloud hung above the treeline. Rachel would come round eventually. It was just that she'd run out of patience. That was his dad's fault, for insisting that he redecorate their house.

'I'm not having them taking over our lives,' Rachel had railed.

'I know,' he'd said.

'Tell them, then.'

'Wouldn't it be better coming from you?'

'God, you're such a coward.'

He slid his fingers across the mousepad and began to trawl the photos he'd recently downloaded. Where had he filed that picture?

He closed the front door, shutting out the ice-sharp night. Kicking off his shoes, he twisted the key in the lock, then moved into the lounge. A sliver of light crept through a crack in the door and arced over the arm of the sofa. He pushed through into the kitchen. Rachel was sitting at the table, a stack of papers in front of her.

He walked across, draped an arm round her shoulder and planted a kiss on the top of her head. The school smell lingered in her hair. 'What are you up to?' he asked, peering down at a scrawl-filled page.

'Mocks,' she said. 'Understanding the text.'

He deposited his bag on a vacant chair. 'Which texts?'

'*Midsummer Night's Dream* and *The Crucible*.'

He took off his coat, dropped it onto his bag. 'Have you eaten?'

'Not yet,' she said, yawning.

'Soup?' he suggested, optimistically.

'God, not again,' she groaned. 'Let's have a takeaway.'

'You don't want soup?' He feigned a wounded rejection.

'Chinese?' she suggested.

'The usual?' he asked, pulling his phone from his pocket. He scrolled through his contacts as he drifted into the lounge. Sinking onto the sofa, he dialled the number and waited. The curtains were still open, the kitchen's hanging bulb mirrored in the window.

After he'd placed the order, he sat staring at the reflections in the black glass.

Rachel ambled in. 'How long?' she asked. She sat on the arm of the sofa, and swivelled towards him, lifting her feet onto the seat.

'An hour.'

'You're not actually going tomorrow, are you?' she asked, folding her arms across her knees.

'Where?' He glanced up at her.

'Your mum and dad's.'

'I don't know.' He looked back at the window.

'So you are, then.'

Sean shrugged, stuck out his lower lip.

'Jesus, Sean, when are you going to stand up to them?'

'It's family.'

'So?'

'I'll just put in an appearance.'

Outside, someone with a torch was walking past.

'They don't even like you.'

'I think that's a bit of an overstatement. They don't understand me is probably more accurate.'

'It's the same thing.'

'Is it?'

'You know you're going to have to assert yourself. It's about making a choice.'

He vented a long sigh. 'Is this the "it's them or me" conversation?'

'Do you like the way they treat you?'

'They're not that bad.'

'Is there something comforting about it? Like Stockholm syndrome.'

He laughed quietly. 'It'll be different this time.'

'You know not making a decision is still a choice.'

He clasped his hands behind his head. 'Do go on, Mrs Freud.'

'I'm trying to make you see sense.'

'I won't go again after this.'

'But you're still going! After everything we said.'

He looked across at her. 'Why don't you come with me?' She was shaking her head at him. 'Anyway,' he said, 'I think I've got a pretty decent painting on the way.'

'Don't change the subject,' she laughed.

They were still talking it over when the takeaway arrived.

The next morning, Sean lingered in the shower, savouring the water's warmth against the back of his neck. He was knuckling a sketch on the shower cubicle's steamed-up door. He would have two men facing out towards the viewer, and one in profile, as though in discussion. That would work, would draw the viewer into the painting. He wiped the sketch away with the edge of his hand, then, closing his eyes, tilted back his head so the water doused his hair. He wished Rachel would ease up about his family. It wasn't as if he wanted to see them anyway.

Cranking off the water, he stepped out of the shower. He picked the towel from the hook on the door and began drying himself. It was as if he wasn't quite one of them any more. Like when Michael was organising his wedding, he wasn't asked to be best man. He hadn't really minded that, but he wasn't even an usher.

'I just think someone a bit more reliable might be better,' Michael had said. 'You know what I mean, don't you?'

He lifted his foot onto the toilet seat and rubbed his leg. Someone more reliable. What had that meant? But he hadn't said anything, hadn't wanted to make waves. Doubling forward, he began to dry between his toes. He didn't actually care about not being an usher. But it was one of those things that had stuck; it was symptomatic of something.

He moved through into the bedroom then paused and pushed his head through the neck of his sweater. He crossed the room and pulled open a drawer, fished out a pair of socks, then sank onto the edge of the bed, the mattress sagging under his weight. Turning, he teased back the duvet slightly. Rachel was lying on her side, facing him, a swathe of black hair trailing out on the pillow behind her.

'Morning,' he said.

She flopped onto her back, smiling, her eyes still closed.

He fingered a strand of hair from her cheek. 'Are you sure you don't want to come with me?'

She rolled away from him and hauled up the duvet so it covered her face.

He watched her for a moment, then bent and pulled on his socks.

The tarmac droned under the tyres, the faster traffic zipped past in the outside lane. Away to the left, behind the bare trees, a smoke plume rose as the steam train shuttled along its restored stretch of track. He wondered if his parents had forgiven him for Christmas yet, the week in a St Ives cottage that Rachel booked. Probably not. He would just have to brave it out. They'd get over it eventually. He swung left at the roundabout, nosed the corner by the cricket pitch then swept past the leisure centre. Apparently, they had a naturist swimming club there once a month. If he could gain access to that it would make a magnificent painting. Had it been done?

He pootled under the old railway bridge and turned toward the town centre. Just after the Conservative Club he dipped left onto a side street, avoiding the one-way system. Cutting up Ackender Road, he detoured onto Kingsland and slowed, leaning forward, his forearms on the wheel. There, on the corner by the row of lock-ups, were the twin telegraph poles they'd used as goal posts during their after-school kick-abouts. There had been a gang of them, Rob Scott, the Brooks boys, Matthew and David. David was deputy head at a school in Woking now; Matthew was a salesman, or something like that. He didn't know what Rob did. By all accounts, he still lived locally, had a wife and two kids. But they'd lost touch, had probably become different people. He drove on round the corner.

He turned onto the Basingstoke road, then immediately

slid a wheel onto the kerb outside a run of mock-Tudor semis. He stared up at the house, its high, shared apex. A faded, almost transparent moon hung in the blue sky above.

As he slammed the car door, he looked across to the field over the road. A flock of birds took flight, black silhouettes reeling up, squawking as they receded. He turned and walked along the drive, picking his way between the parked-up cars: his dad's Volvo, Phil's battered VW. Meandering round to the side of the house, he thumbed the latch, closed the gate behind him, then moved along the passage, passing the side entrance to the garage. Outside the back door, he paused, inhaled a long, chill breath, and slowly breathed it out. Then he pushed into the kitchen.

Angela, his mother, was kneeling in front of the multi-fuel burner by the far wall. She was rattling a poker in the grate, riddling out the extinct ashes. Phil, her brother, was standing near her, gazing down at the slate-tiled floor and pinching his chin meditatively.

'…they're all bent anyway,' Phil said.

'Hello you two,' Sean said, leaning the door closed.

From an armchair by a window in the extension, Bella, the old boxer dog, offered an enquiring grunt, then raised her head.

Angela shuffled round on her knees, still gripping the poker. She was wearing a yellow sweater, black slacks; a tuft of hair was sticking up at the front. 'Hello, Sean,' she said, tugging up a drooping sleeve. 'Rachel not with you?'

'She couldn't make it,' Sean apologised. 'She sends her love.'

'...and Martin and Bridget are the worst of the lot,' Phil complained.

There was a dull thump from across the kitchen. Bella was padding over, stiff-legged. As she neared she began to squirm, excited, arthritic, her tail frantically wagging.

'The whole system's crooked,' Phil continued. 'It's the bloody Tories.'

Bella hopped up on her hind legs so that Sean caught her front paws. He eased her down to the floor again then knelt and rubbed under her ear so she leaned her head into the pressure. Angela was riddling out the ash with renewed vigour. Phil folded his arms, bounced on the balls of his feet. There was something different about him. He'd grown paunchy for one thing.

'They're selling this town down the river. Destroying it...'

It was the moustache, Sean realised. Phil had always had a moustache. Perhaps shaving it off had been some sort of reaction to his wife leaving him for her line manager.

Angela opened the burner's lower door and cautiously dragged out the ash-filled tray. She meticulously tipped its contents into a plastic bag then slid the tray back into the drawer and joggled it roughly.

'...and all these people did was complain it'd disturb the dormice. Dormice!' Phil smiled bitterly, was shaking his head at Sean.

Sean patted the dog's side. Was he supposed to say

something? He stood.

'Do you think the people they're up against give a shit about dormice?' Phil was staring at Sean now, waiting.

Sean felt himself flush. 'Sorry, who doesn't give a shit about dormice?' he asked.

'The developers, Sean,' Phil snapped, scowling.

'Right.'

'And Fight for Sudleigh roll over so they don't hinder Bridget's ascent up the greasy pole. It's pathetic.'

Sean watched Bella amble back across the kitchen. She clambered slowly onto her chair, then circled twice and settled again.

'Little deals and backhanders. It's all completely bent...'

Angela tied off the plastic bag, then, with a hand on the stove's top, pressed herself to her feet. 'Terrible,' she said, moving across the kitchen. She disappeared outside, leaving the door open behind her so the cold air flooded in.

'I had to step away,' Phil explained, scratching his cheek, his fingers rasping against his stubble. 'No other choice.'

Sean looked at Phil and wondered what he was talking about. Then, Angela was back in the kitchen.

'So, how are you, Mum?' Sean asked as she scurried past him.

She hesitated, turned. 'You couldn't do me a favour, could you?'

'What's that?' Sean asked.

'Could you make the fire while I get cleaned up?' She

tugged up a sleeve.

He frowned at her.

'The paper's there.' She nodded at the stack of old newspapers in the corner by the burner. 'The wood's in the garage.' She blew upwards, trying to cool a gathering sweat, then pulled open the door into the hallway.

'Right,' Sean said, watching the door swing closed behind her.

Phil strode across to the window by the dog's chair, stared out. Beyond him, in the garden, a blackbird flitted between the whitebeam's bare branches.

Bending, Sean picked a *Sudleigh Gazette* from the pile and dropped it onto the top of the burner. 'Permission Granted for New Development', the headline proclaimed. He separated the outermost sheet, rolled it roughly, and tied it in a knot. Stooping, he threw it into the firebox then plucked off another sheet. He could hear water running in the cloakroom next door.

'The planning system actually works against the interests of the people…' Phil said.

Sean shook his head and tossed the twisted page into the burner.

'So, how's Rachel?' Angela asked, edging back in through the door.

'Shattered, I think. Marking mocks.' He rolled another sheet.

Angela nodded. 'Is she?' she said, unconvinced. 'And how

are you getting on?' She was smoothing out a crease in her jumper with the flat of her hand.

'Pretty well, actually. I've got an exhibition up in London. Brick Lane.'

Phil angled his paunch toward the conversation.

'That's brilliant, Sean,' Angela said, her eyes lighting. 'You must be excited.'

Phil stepped towards them. 'Did I tell you Liam got through his interview with Deutsche Bank?' He planted his hands on his hips and rolled his shoulders.

'That's wonderful, Phil,' Angela said. 'That's two pieces of good news then.' She smiled at Sean.

Sean leaned down and tossed the coiled paper into the burner. Liam was his sainted cousin; he'd recently completed a PhD at Cambridge.

'Quantitative strategist,' Phil said. 'Calculating risk or something.'

Sean tied off another sheet of paper and pitched it into the burner.

'I mean,' Phil continued, 'I've always said to Liam, the money they're moving around, it's not real, is it? It's just numbers on a computer screen.'

Sean screwed the last sheet into a ball, threw it into the firebox then walked across the kitchen.

'...but they're going to pay him ninety K, so who cares?' Phil continued. 'I mean...'

Outside, the morning air was still brittle. Sean stalled by

the door into the garage, was staring at the sloping top of the brick-built coal bunker against the wall beyond the gate.

It had snowed one year; he must only have been four or five, Michael would have been eight or nine. They'd been playing out, building a snowman on the driveway. Then, Michael had disappeared; Sean hadn't seen him go. He'd called out but Michael didn't answer, so he'd trudged back up to the house. Then, as he was scuffing in through the back gate, an avalanche dropped on his head. Michael had climbed up onto the coal bunker, had been lying in wait. The snow had gone down the back of his anorak, had filled his wellies. He'd started to cry and Michael had roared with laughter. He'd forgotten about that.

Sean pulled open the door into the garage and stepped inside. There was a tall bookcase lying across a pair of trestles. John, his father, was bending over it, gripping a tin of wood-stain in one hand and a brush in the other. The air was filled with the stain's sweet acridity.

'Alright, Dad?'

'Rachel not with you?' John glanced up then dipped the brush, and worked the stain along the side panel's grain. He always had some chore ongoing. It was how he'd filled his time since taking early retirement a couple of years ago.

Sean smiled slightly. 'No, she had to work. She's sorry she couldn't come.'

John snorted.

Sean looked around the garage. It was crammed with items

his father deemed essential: shelves of assorted paint he'd been unable to part with for decades; chests of tools from his brief career as a mechanic. There was a long wooden bench with a weighty vice on it; racks of plastic tubs rose up the wall behind. Over by the garage door there was an antique trolley jack, its yellow handle standing erect.

'Least she could have done was come today,' John said, 'after missing Christmas.'

'She wanted to be here...'

'We always spend Christmas together,' John said, dipping his brush again.

'We just needed to get away, Dad. Rachel needed to recharge.' Sean spied the wood-filled bucket on the floor by the dented freezer.

'Michael and Joanne managed to come,' John added.

Sean shrugged, refusing to apologise. 'So where's the bookcase going?'

'Front room.'

Sean waited for more information but John just continued to apply the stain. Stepping across, Sean crouched and gathered a bundle of splintery kindling, then stood again, cradling the wood in the crook of his arm. He eyed his father's blue knee-length overall, the grey, thinning hair that barely concealed the emerging bald spot. 'Did I tell you I've got an exhibition in London?'

John worked the stain with long, slick strokes. 'You getting paid for it?'

'It's not really like that.' Sean moved across to the door.

'You can lie in the gutter for nothing,' John said, tilting his head and eyeing his work.

'Right,' Sean sighed. He elbowed out of the garage, buttocked the door shut then hesitated. You can lie in the gutter for nothing. He chewed over the sentence, rolled it round his mind. That was a new one. It was like the time when he explained he wanted to go to university to study art. He'd just applied to the Slade School.

'And where's that going to get you?' his dad had said.

'It's what I want to do.'

'What you want to do?' John had scoffed. 'I used to love being a mechanic. I wanted my own garage. But I had to give up on that dream, didn't I?'

Sean shook his head then ferried the wood into the kitchen. Phil was standing by the window, looking out; Angela was absent somewhere. Kneeling, he tipped the wood onto the floor then reached into the stove and pressed the paper into an even bed. He was layering the wood on top of it when the back door swung open and slammed against the pine worktop. John entered at a gallop, his overall jettisoned. He blustered through to the hallway.

Sean could hear indistinct voices. He glanced across. Bella winked open an eye, then closed it again and nuzzled her chin against her front paws. Turning slowly, Phil poked a finger in his ear and waggled it so his unbuttoned shirt cuff flapped.

Angela bustled in, two coats hanging over her arm. 'Your

dad's got them in the lounge,' she said. 'I should get back in there before he says something untoward.' She sucked in a cheek comically. 'Can you run these upstairs?' She extended her laden arm toward Sean.

'Too good for the cloakroom, are they?' Phil said, staring down at his fingertip.

'Shut up, Philip,' Angela hissed.

Phil looked up innocently. 'What?'

'Where do you want them?' Sean stood, took the coats.

'Just dump them in Michael's room. On the bed'll do.' She withdrew.

Sean stared at the coats then looked across at Phil. 'What's this all about, Phil?' he asked.

Phil shrugged and turned towards the window. 'Always been bad chemistry in this family,' he said toward the glass. 'It's why Anne never wanted to...'

Sean edged into the murky hallway. Only a second-hand light filtered down from the window on the landing. He paused among the shadows at the base of the stairs, listening.

'No, it runs like a dream,' Michael was saying.

'I've never seen the point in them,' John countered. 'Not unless you're a farmer.'

'That's lovely,' Angela said. 'Is it cashmere?'

Sean quietly scaled the stairs. At the top, he turned right into Michael's old room. There was a wardrobe with mirrored doors across from the bed by the wall. Michael used to lift his weights in front of those mirrors, considering his biceps. Sean lobbed the coats at the bed and retreated.

Out on the landing he lingered by the window, resting his hands on the sill. He leaned his head close to the cool glass and stared at the shiny new Range Rover parked behind his own jaded heap. Typical Mike. He was a quantity surveyor. A proper job, his dad called it.

He turned and sauntered along the landing to his old room. All the posters on the walls were gone, his prints of the classics, Van Gogh, Monet and the rest. The carpet had been pulled up and replaced with laminate flooring. His father had become infatuated with laminate a year or so ago. He'd been able to get it cheap somewhere, so he'd bought in bulk. He'd run through Sean's room, the front lounge, and the master bedroom before Angela had issued a cease and desist. But he'd had some left. Which was why he'd wanted to install it at their place.

Sean ran a hand through his curly hair, held the back of his neck. Virtually everything of his had gone now, his traces removed. There was just his old hi-fi on top of the drawers by his bed. He wandered across and pressed the CD player's eject button. It didn't respond. He opened the cassette deck but it was empty. He closed it again then sidled across to the window.

He gazed out at the run of house backs through the mesh of naked tree branches. Somehow, he couldn't picture his younger self looking out and seeing this view; couldn't feel what his old self felt. Was that normal? It's what eight years away does, he supposed. He'd hardly stayed in touch when he was in London. Chewing the inside of his lip, he stared down at the frost-grey lawn, at the brown patches where Bella repeatedly squatted. But it was the way they treated him... And the way he complied. It was bizarre. He was their skivvy somehow, bottom of the pile; make the fire, put the coats away. Had it always been like this? From the room below, his mother's voice rose, becoming shrill. Perhaps it was going wrong already.

He walked back across the room, his soles gummily sucking off the laminate.

*

He pushed into the lounge. The heat was almost overwhelming. There was a fire in the grate, the banked coals a molten amber mass. John was slouching in an armchair by the brick hearth, his fingers interlocked across his belly, his legs outstretched. Michael and Joanne were occupying the sofa in the bay, the window behind them bright where the January sun struck the skim of winter grime on the glass. Michael's body-built bulk was obvious; beside him, Joanne looked tiny. Her blond hair was pulled back into a pony-tail. Angela was sitting on the edge of the armchair beside Joanne, their knees almost touching.

'Alright, bro?' Michael said, beaming broadly.

'How are you both?' Sean enquired.

Angela turned towards him suddenly, her hands clasped on her knee. She looked like she was about to cry. 'I'm going to be a grandma.'

'Congratulations,' Sean said. He looked across at Michael and Joanne. 'Congratulations, you two.' He tried to think of something else to say but couldn't, so he puckered a thin smile.

'Was it planned, then?' John asked, crossing his feet.

'John!' Angela gasped.

'We've been thinking about it for a while, haven't we?' Joanne said.

'And now I've got my promotion,' Michael added, 'Jo can take some time out.'

'But I'll want to get back to work fairly soon,' Joanne said, patting his hand.

Sean leaned back against the radiator, watching.

'...and we'd really like you to be hands-on grandparents,' Joanne said to Angela.

'Oh, we'd love that,' Angela said. She glanced warily at John.

'You're still young enough to enjoy it,' Michael said. 'All the pleasure and none of the responsibility.'

'I did my time with children,' John said sourly. Angela glared at him.

Sean tried not to smile.

'And we're thinking of getting a dog,' Michael announced obliquely.

Angela leaned forward, looking round Joanne. 'Won't that

be too much, the training? At the same time.'

'We'll get it before the baby arrives,' Michael explained.

'Then we'll have the full set,' Joanne added.

'It's so exciting,' Angela said.

Sean watched her stand and wrap her arms round Joanne's neck.

'I'm so proud of you both,' she said, straightening again. She turned and looked at Sean, narrowing her eyes affectionately. 'Do you fancy making a cuppa, love?'

Sean shook his head, laughed slightly. 'Not really, no.'

'I'll have one if you're making,' Michael said.

Angela sat again. 'So have you thought about names?'

'It's a bit early for that,' Michael protested.

'I've always liked Aubrey,' John mused.

'Aubrey?' Sean laughed.

Joanne tittered.

John was staring at Sean. 'What's wrong with Aubrey?' he said.

Sean shrugged. 'Nothing.' He looked from face to face, but no one was paying him any attention.

'What about Philip?' Angela suggested.

'I quite like Jack,' Michael said.

'Jack's nice…'

Sean pulled open the door and drifted out into the hallway. Smiling wryly, he pushed through to the kitchen.

Phil was resting an elbow on the worktop near the cooker, was tapping the screen of his smartphone. 'It's like getting blood from a stone,' he said.

Sean stepped towards the burner, squatted and stuffed in the remaining wood. Standing again, he moved across to the back door.

'I've put in an FOI about the new development...' Phil began.

Sean strode towards the coal bunker, gripped the shovel's short wooden handle and scooped up a load.

'...asking if there was contact between the developers and the council...' Phil was standing in the doorway, prodding his smartphone. He backed into the kitchen as Sean approached.

Sean ferried the coal across to the multi-burner and fed in the nuggets.

'...they're just fudging round it...'

Sean carried the shovel back outside, leaned it against the coal bunker and returned.

'I'm going to have to escalate it to the ICO. Openness and transparency, isn't it?'

'Definitely,' Sean said, walking across to the drawer by the sink. He dragged it open and extracted a box of matches then pushed the drawer closed. He looked at Phil. 'They've made the big announcement.'

Phil glanced up from his phone. 'What big announcement?'

'Joanne's pregnant.'

Phil nodded. 'Is she?' He said it as though a long suspected plot had just been revealed.

'Apparently.' Sean crossed the kitchen. 'And they're getting a puppy.'

'Why?'

'You should go through.' He knelt in front of the burner.

'What for?'

He turned and looked back at his uncle. 'Offer your congratulations, maybe.'

'Right. Yeah.' Phil sniffed then stood straight. He moved towards the door into the hallway. 'Wish me luck,' he said, edging from the room.

Sean pinched a couple of matches from the box then dragged the brown tips across the friction pad until they spat into ignition. He held the wavering flame to the paper until it caught, then moved the matches along and lit another corner. Slowly, the orange glow spread. There was a crackle from the wood, a resiny pop, then flames licked up through the coals. A low roar grew as the early flames were drawn up the flue. A waft of smoke snorted out as he closed the front. For a moment he listened to the intensifying roar, then he stood and walked across to where Bella was softly snoring, caught in a dream.

As he sat on the edge of her chair, she winked open an eye. She sat up gradually, her warm sleeping smell rising with her. Raising her grey chin, she stretched, dignified. He stroked her soft, warm head and stared at her grey muzzle. She was an old dog now. She leaned forward, pressed her head to his cheek and licked his nose.

'Thanks, Bella,' he said, and he felt the tears well. He pulled her toward him and kissed the top of her head then he stood. She was looking up at him, watching him knowingly. He stroked beneath her ear for a while then patted her.

'Bye, Bella,' he said.

With the flames howling up the chimney, he crossed the kitchen and stepped outside. He pulled the door closed behind him.

★

At home, the curtains in the lounge hadn't been opened. He climbed the stairs. From the bedroom doorway he could see Rachel was still in bed. He walked through to the spare room, pulled open the desk drawer and picked out a sketchbook, a couple of pencils. He riffled through the sketchbook until he found the empty pages at the back, then padded into the bedroom.

Quietly, he walked across and pulled open a crack in the curtains for light to leak in. There was a stand-back chair over in the corner. He carried it round to Rachel's side of the bed and sat, watching her. She was lying on her back, one arm sprawled over the top of the duvet. He listened to her breathing for a while, then he began to draw her, her sleeping peace.

She woke after a while, made a clacking sound with her tongue then slowly opened her eyes.

'What are you doing?' she asked.

'Just drawing.'

A slow smile lit her face. She lifted a hand and rubbed her nose. 'How was it?'

'Oh, you know.'

'What happened?'

'The usual,' he said. He closed the sketchbook and dropped it onto the floor along with the pencils. He kneeled onto the bed, then flopped over her and slid to his side. 'Joanne's pregnant.'

Rachel laughed huskily. 'That'll please your mum and dad.'

Sean peeled back the covers, then pulled them over himself and hunkered down so his head was on the pillow beside her. He stared up at the ceiling.

'You've still got your clothes on,' she said, looking across at him.

TONY & LYDIA
(AGAIN)

He was still at work.

Tony stood by the window behind his desk, prodding at the screen of his mobile phone. There was an email in his private account. It had arrived while he was teaching his last seminar. He opened the message and skimmed the contents.

'*Thank you for giving us the opportunity to read…not right for our list…wish you luck finding a home… Kind Regards…*'

He gazed out through the window. The day was fading now; the light had already thinned. Students walked the paths, drifting towards the halls of residence, the cluster of grim brown tower blocks that dominated the view. In the distance, the lights of the nearby town glimmered and pulsed.

So that was it. *The Jazz Cats* was sunk. Not a single publisher had expressed any interest after six months of submissions. He slid the phone into his jeans pocket. It was entirely possible, he decided, that *The Jazz Cats* was too sophisticated for the current cultural climate.

'Ah, Tony,' a voice said. 'Just the man.'

Tony looked across. Glenn was in the doorway. He was the new head of department, forty-four, moustachioed, and wearing heavy-framed spectacles.

Tony picked his coat from the back of the chair. 'Hello, Glenn.'

'Did you get a chance to read my email?' Glenn asked, stepping into the room.

Tony slid an arm into a sleeve. 'Sorry, I've been completely swamped.'

Glenn was surveying the crowded bookshelves, his hands in his cardigan pockets. 'We should discuss your research plans at some point,' he said, turning. 'It's nearly three years since you published.'

Tony zipped up his coat. He needed to escape. Glenn had been trying to schedule a meeting for the past two weeks.

'Are you working on anything at the moment?'

Tony bent, gathered his leather satchel from the floor by the desk and straightened. 'I am, actually, yes,' he lied. He hung the satchel strap over his shoulder.

'That's very exciting,' Glenn said.

'It is,' Tony agreed, widening his eyes as he crossed the room.

'So, what is it? The new project.'

Tony flipped the light-switch, moved out into the corridor. 'I suppose, in many ways...' he singled out his office key from the bunch and turned, '...it's about modern life.'

Glenn sauntered out, stood beside him. 'I really don't like having to do this whole hassling thing,' he said. 'But it's the job.'

Tony pulled the door shut, locked it.

'You see, things'll start getting a bit tricky if you don't publish something soon.'

'Honestly, Glenn,' Tony said, trying the handle, 'there's nothing to worry about.' He pocketed his keys and began to back away.

'Management have said we can't afford to carry any "passengers".' Glenn made quote marks with his fingers.

'Sorry, but I really do need to...' Tony tilted his head to one side by way of explanation.

'Can you send me a research plan?'

Tony held up a hand, retreating still. 'Absolutely,' he said, then spun away.

'By the end of the week,' Glenn called as Tony scurried along the corridor.

★

Tony pushed his front door shut, scuffed his feet on the mat. He paused for a moment and sniffed. There was a smell in the house, a sour, insistent tang.

He would need to wash up at some point, empty the bin. He'd let things slide in the last month, since Lydia stopped staying over. All he'd done was forget her birthday. 'Indicative of our relationship,' she'd said, among other things. In the kitchen at the far end of the hallway, the boiler fired into life; its metal casing rattled. No, he couldn't think about that Lydia stuff now. He needed to conjure up a project.

He climbed the stairs two at a time. On the landing, he elbowed into his study, turned on the light and deposited his satchel on the floor. He peeled off his coat, slung it onto the wicker basket in the corner. Sitting on his old office chair, he opened the notepad that lay on the desk. He flipped through to an empty page then reached across and picked a pencil from the jar on the windowsill.

*

An hour later, Tony leaned back and re-read the list.

Detective. Baz Rudge. Bipolar/anxiety issues.

Historical fiction – Rewrite a real life? Rasputin's daughter??
   Musical?

Novel – lecturer in throes of mid-life crisis.

None of them excited him. They weren't even original. He gazed idly at the shelves along the wall, the book spines facing him. The problem was he didn't have the space to think. If Glenn wasn't harassing him, it was a student wanting advice, or Lydia making demands. It was desiccating his creativity.

But he'd written *The Jazz Cats*, hadn't he? What he needed to do was trust his talent. He nodded, in agreement. So, what to write? What was popular at…

In the hallway, the front door thumped shut.

'Tony?' Lydia called. After a moment, the stairs creaked.

'Yes,' he said, screwing his eyes shut.

She arrived on the landing, rubbing her hands together. 'What are you doing?'

'I was trying to work.' He tossed the pad onto the desk, turned.

'I've been waiting for you.'

He frowned, uncertain. 'OK?'

'You know how important this is to me, don't you?'

She must be talking about In Bloom, her pitch to the council. She'd been banging on about it for weeks. Was he supposed to have gone round?

'You promised you'd help.'

'Right.' He slapped his hands onto the armrests and pushed himself to his feet. 'Shall we go through it now then?' He held her gaze.

'Not if you're going to have that attitude, no.'

'I don't have an attitude. I'm happy to help.'

She shook her head minutely. 'Fine.' She turned.

He followed her down the stairs, tracked her into the lounge. She was standing by the armchair, unbuttoning her overcoat.

'You know it smells in here, don't you?' she said.

He walked across to the bay window. The lights were on in the houses opposite; the streetlamp's glow reflected dully on the frost-skimmed car roofs. He dragged the curtains closed.

'It wouldn't hurt to clean up once in a while.'

He crossed to the sofa, sat and slouched back. 'Do you want me to help or not?'

She settled on the armchair, pulled a piece of paper from her coat pocket. 'You are going to do this properly, aren't you?'

He raised his chin, scratched his neck. 'What am I looking for?'

'Tone, argument, that sort of thing,' she said, unfolding the sheet of paper.

He nodded and contemplated the mantelpiece. On the right-hand side was a squat glass block with green streaks layered through. *Ferns Interned*, she called it. She'd begun importing her artworks when she started staying over; to make the place more homely, she'd said.

She cleared her throat. 'Are you ready?'

'Fire away.'

'Ladies and gentleman of the council,' she began, 'Sudleigh is a wonderful place to live. However, these are divided times. There are divisions in society, and in the community. We need to do something to bring the town, and its people, together. But how can this be achieved? The answer is both obvious and affordable. By running an In Bloom competition...'

Tony's mind was drifting. Perhaps he could still use *The Jazz Cats* idea, but turn it on its head. Make the Jazz Cats the heroes rather than the criminals. They could solve the crimes. Maybe there was rumour of a gang up the street grooming kittens. No, he had to stop thinking about *The Jazz Cats*. He tried to focus on what Lydia was saying.

'...small investment from the council, we can celebrate Sudleigh and show it at its best. There is already a great deal of interest in participation from...'

He needed to come up with something new, something substantial. A novel. But how was he supposed to work with Glenn pressuring him? University hadn't always been like that. But everything changed. Like Lydia. It had all been so uncomplicated when they first started out. He glanced at her.

'...Ladies and gentlemen of the council, we humbly beseech you to support this project. All we ask is a meagre two thousand pounds. And with that money we will not only make Sudleigh glorious, but we will bring the community together.'

How were a few hanging baskets going to heal Sudleigh's social divisions? It was naïve at...

'What do you think?' Lydia said.

'Hmm?' He looked across. She was watching him. 'Yes, it's good,' he hazarded.

She reached into her coat, pulled out a pencil. 'Anything I need to change?'

'Well...' He puckered his lips, trying to recall the scraps he'd heard. 'I would just be careful you don't, you know, over-promise.'

Fine lines creased her forehead. 'Over-promise?'

'You know, saying In Bloom will bring people together…'

'But that's the whole point of In Bloom, isn't it?'

'I like it,' he said. 'I really do. But maybe just say it once and push the 'celebrate the town' angle a bit more.'

She jotted something, the paper crinkling against her thigh. 'Anything else?'

'Well, I did wonder…' He rubbed the side of his nose with a finger. 'Does 'humbly beseech' sound a bit High Anglican?'

Her eyes narrowed. 'I'm asking if the argument's OK. Not for a textual analysis.'

'It's perfect, then. Is that what you want me to say?'

She straightened, folded the piece of paper. 'This is the problem, isn't it?'

'Oh God,' he said, leaning back his head.

'You're not interested.'

'I am interested,' he countered, without enthusiasm.

'No, you're not. It's always got to be about you, hasn't it, Tony?'

He stared blankly at the wall above the mantelpiece. There was a brighter patch of wallpaper where a mirror had hung for years. His previous girlfriend had taken it when she left.

'You know a relationship is an exchange. There's got to be give and take.'

'Yes, I'm aware how relationships work, thank you.'

'Are you, though?' She folded the piece of paper again, dragged her fingers along the crease. 'Look,' she said, business-like now, 'I think we need to talk.'

'Can we not do this now?' He saw her jaw clench. 'It's just that Glenn's been…'

'There's always an excuse, isn't there?'

He raised his hands, massaged his forehead and eyes.

'You do realise this avoidance of confrontation is learned behaviour, don't you?'

'I'm not avoiding confrontation. I have to do some work. That's all it is.' He let his arms fall to his sides, looked at her.

She was buttoning up her coat. 'Probably stems from your childhood, your parents' relationship.'

'I'm trying to salvage my career, Lydia.'

She leaned towards him. 'And I'm trying to launch In Bloom.'

'They're a bit different though, aren't they?'

Her eyes hardened. 'Why're they different? Hmm?'

'Please, Lydia. Can't we just talk tomorrow?'

She held out a hand, palm up. 'It's the In Bloom committee tomorrow. I've told you this.'

'Right,' he said irritably, 'if you want to talk now, let's talk.'

'Oh, don't bother,' she said. She stood, shook her head, then strode across the room.

'What have I done wrong now?' he shouted.

In the hallway, the front door slammed.

★

At work the next day, Tony was sitting at his desk, the strip light bright overhead. Resting his chin on the heel of his hand, he stared at the computer screen.

'Dear Glenn,' the email began. And that's where it ended. He'd become distracted.

'It's always got to be about you.' That's what Lydia had said. After she'd made him listen to her In Bloom speech. He'd given his advice, tried to help. And had she appreciated it?

Out in the corridor, the happy gabble of students came and went. He sat back. The danger was he risked becoming like Dennis O'Hare. Dennis was fifty-six, a novelist who'd taught at the university for twenty-five years. His two previous books remained unpublished.

One morning last week, Tony was arriving at work when he'd seen Dennis' office door was open. As he passed he'd glimpsed Dennis hunched over his desk, head in hands. He was still wearing his bicycle clips. Tony had leaned into the room. 'Everything OK, Dennis?' he'd asked.

Dennis had turned and fixed him with a mournful gaze. 'I've no more words,' he'd said, then slowly swivelled away again.

No, Tony wasn't at that point yet. But he needed to focus on his writing. And that was impossible when Lydia was consistently spelling out his psychological defects. How had that ever helped anyone? He was still shaking his head when someone knocked at the door. He peered over the top of his monitor then squinted, as though in pain, when the knock came again.

'Come in,' he called.

The door opened and Greta edged into the room. She was one of the PhD students he supervised. Fifty-three and pale, she was wearing a faux-fur coat.

She tossed her waxy, red-tinted hair. 'I wasn't sure you were here.'

Tony clicked the mouse, accessed his calendar. He browsed the entry for 3.30. *Greta. PhD. Read attachment.*

'I'm a bit early,' she said, advancing towards the chair opposite.

'What were we discussing?' He scrolled through his inbox.

'My draft board submission. I sent it to you last week.'

'Of course,' he said, locating her email.

'I don't think there's too much wrong with it,' she asserted.

He double-clicked the mouse to open the attachment. 'OK. Bear with me.' He skimmed the opening lines.

'She drew the curtains and looked out over the rooftops towards the snow-crusted hills on the other side of the bay. Why had she come to Reykjavik of all places? But after the funeral she'd needed to get away. And remembering the funeral, with her father lying there, in his favourite pin-striped suit, she began to sob...'

That was it. She was writing an autobiographical novel about her grief after her father's death.

'I think you're making good progress,' he said.

'I've never had a problem writing,' she stated, pulling a notepad from her bag. 'It's the benefit of having been a journalist for so many years.'

Tony smiled. She always found a way to mention her journalistic past. She'd been the local politics reporter for the *Rutland Herald*.

'Actually,' he said, 'could you give me ten minutes? I should really finish this email.' He nodded at the monitor.

'That's all right,' she said. 'I'll grab a tea.' She moved towards the door. 'Do you want anything? Cake?' She looked back and grinned at him.

'I'm fine, thanks.' He watched the door close behind her. Maybe he should write a memoir. He could always fabricate a traumatic childhood. That sort of thing usually sold. It was definitely worth considering.

He focused on the screen and read on.

...fat tears falling. Never again would she see him. Never again would she hold...

★

As the bus pulled away, Tony veered from the pavement and struck out across the unlit green. The cold had sharpened; the grass was crisp with frost. Pulling his hands up into his sleeves, he walked on, the steady drone of passing traffic receding behind him.

He would come straight out with it. He'd say, 'There's a point in every relationship when you have to assess if it's working.' She'd probably start analysing him, but he'd stand firm. 'I'm still very fond of you,' he'd say. That was nice. 'But I think we both know that we want different things…' He just needed to make it sound like it was what she wanted.

He strode beneath the bare-branched beech trees along the green's fringe, crossed the dead-end access road. The lights were on in Lydia's, upstairs and down. He advanced up the brief brickwork path, fished his keys from his pocket, let himself into the house. Wiping his feet on the coir mat, he gently closed the door. Voices were leaking from the lounge, muted.

He moved along the hallway, passed into the bright kitchen. There was a tray on the worktop, beside the kettle. It was loaded with teapot, milk jug, sugar bowl, cups and spoons. Behind the tray was an old, battered Family Circle biscuit tin. He drifted across to the serving hatch and lingered there, listening.

'…and the WI want to do something with the plot down by the train station…'

He'd forgotten about the meeting.

'I'll get the tea. Miriam's brought cake if anyone can be tempted.'

'It's a bit of an experiment.'

'…make a feature of the roundabout…'

'…mainly dates.'

There were footsteps in the hallway. Tony leaned back against the worktop, hitched his satchel strap up his shoulder.

Lydia materialised, pulling up the sleeves of her white cotton blouse. She fixed him with a look, then bristled past and set the kettle to boil. She studied his reflection in the window for a moment.

'What are you doing here, Tony?'

'I thought we should talk.'

The kettle crackled into life.

She opened the fridge, bent, retrieved a carton of milk, swung the door shut. 'I'm in the middle of a meeting,' she said, looking at him, incredulous.

'Even so,' he insisted, 'there are things I think we need to discuss.'

On the other side of the kitchen, the cat flap rattled. Eddie the cat clambered in. He eyed Tony for a moment, then lifted a front paw and shook it.

The conversation in the lounge continued.

'…it's the way they keep building…'

'…marigolds and pansies would go quite nicely…'

'I think we both know that things between us…' Tony began.

She whipped round. 'I've got guests, Tony,' she whispered fiercely, then turned away again.

He folded his arms, shook his head.

Eddie padded across the kitchen and pushed against Lydia's legs as she poured milk into the jug. 'Yes, I know, Edward.

I'll feed you in a minute,' she said, screwing the cap onto the carton.

'So I should go. Is that what you're saying?'

She prised the lid off the biscuit tin.

He watched her profile. 'You were the one who wanted to talk.'

She pulled a face at the tin's contents.

'What about tomorrow then?'

She lifted her head and stared at the window, his reflection. 'It's my address to council.'

He shrugged. 'That's all right. I'll come with you.'

She laid the tin lid on the worktop. 'You don't have to, Tony.'

The kettle rumbled to a boil, clicked off. She filled the teapot, then pulled open a drawer, took out a knife. Eddie mewed again.

There was movement in the hallway. A short, large-eared man appeared in the doorway. 'All right?' the man said, nodding abruptly at Tony. 'Can I do anything, Lydia?'

Tony was about to make a suggestion.

'You could take this through, if you don't mind, Phil,' Lydia said, lifting the tray, the crockery rattling. She shuffled round and handed it to the man. He withdrew as Lydia turned back to the worktop.

Tony watched her work the knife through the brown mass in the tin.

'I'm obviously in the way,' he said.

'Mmm,' she murmured. Eddie looked up at Tony, flicked his tail and mewed.

'Fine then. We'll talk tomorrow.'

Lydia closed her eyes, shook her head.

He stalked out of the kitchen, along the hall and let himself out of the house. He closed the door heavily behind him, making a point, then he stepped onto the pavement and set off towards the town centre.

The cold was piercing now; the flesh on his face tightened. Settling into a steady rhythm, he was soon past the Conservative Club, the retirement flats. On the road beside him, the evening traffic rubbered by. Yes, he would definitely break up with her tomorrow. And there would be no more of this trying to spare her feelings.

★

He was threading through the after-class stew of bodies in the campus' main square, heading back to the department now his final seminar of the day was done. Jackdaws clattered overhead, returning to their roosting places. Dark, dense clouds were rolling in, gathering. Snow had been forecast.

He passed the large central planter where students sat talking, smoking. The greasy smell of frying burgers hung in the air, leaking from the eatery beside the entrance to Biological Sciences. He navigated a huddle of students outside the shop in the corner, hauled open the heavy door, travelled along the short passageway and scuffed up two flights of dusty stairs.

Moving swiftly along the corridor, he delved into his pocket, retrieved his keys. He was unlocking his office when a door opened further along. Glenn and Vaughan, a recent MA graduate who'd set up his own press, emerged, began ambling towards him.

Tony pushed open his office door, was about to dart inside.

'Hello, Tony,' Glenn called amiably.

Tony glanced at the pair. 'Hello, chaps.' he said. 'You well?' He sidestepped into his office, had started to close the door but then they were there, outside, unavoidable.

'I think so,' Glenn said, pressing his pelvis beyond the plane of his shoulders. 'Been having a little editorial meeting, haven't we?'

'I'm incredibly excited about *Aaargh!*' Vaughan said, smiling, fresh-faced. 'It's really pushing the boundaries.'

'*Aaargh?*' Tony asked.

'Just a little book I've put together,' Glenn confirmed.

'Oh, OK,' Tony said flatly, gripping the door handle.

'It's such a brilliant concept,' Vaughan enthused. 'It explores Glenn's gestation and birth through an extended poetry cycle.'

Tony's eyebrows arched. 'Wow,' he said, and slowly nodded.

'Anyway...' Vaughan pulled back a sleeve, checked his watch, 'I should make a move. I've got a meeting at four.'

Tony began to close the door. 'Good to see you both.'

'You are sending me that outline, aren't you?' Glenn

intervened.

'Absolutely,' Tony said through the narrowing gap.

'And we should discuss your student satisfaction scores.'

'Definitely.' Tony cocked his head to one side. 'I should get on.'

'Just send the outline when you're ready.'

'Will do.' Tony closed the door and turned. Jesus. How had it come to this? Badgered by an experimental poet. And *Aaargh!* God almighty. He gripped the back of his neck and stared out through the window.

*

He walked up the short path to Lydia's front door. A splintery sleet was falling, tapping against his coat, numbing his forehead.

He slotted the key into the lock, edged inside and pressed the door shut behind him. The lights were off in the kitchen, the house was quiet. He dragged a hand down his face, wiping away the water that had run from his hair, then advanced, leaving wet sole-prints on the parquet floor. He looked into the lounge. Eddie was curled on the sofa, asleep or pretending to be.

Tony moved along the hall, started up the stairs. There were pictures hanging on the wall, some of Lydia's bizarre paintings; landscapes, apparently. On the windowsill where the stairs turned, a large blue dish with copper handprints round its edge was displayed. *Unity* she'd called it.

Gaining the landing, he saw the bathroom door was ajar, the light on inside. He approached stealthily, wary of disturbing Lydia's new lodger, an intense Russian girl.

'Lydia?' he said quietly. A trickle of water ran down his cheek.

The door swung back and Lydia was standing there, an eyeliner brush in one hand.

'What do you want, Tony?' she said, returning to the mirror over the sink. She continued applying her eyeliner.

He rested his shoulder against the doorframe. 'I said I'd come and support you.'

'Mmm.' Screwing the cap back onto the bottle, she leaned towards the mirror.

'And I thought we could talk.'

She patted her hair, pressed her lips together then turned towards him, made a shooing gesture with her hands. He backed up and she walked past him, into the bedroom. He followed.

She was pulling on her navy velvet jacket. 'You do realise I'm about to deliver a presentation to the council,' she said, tugging down her sleeves.

'You did mention it, yes.'

She untucked her hair from the collar of her jacket. 'So it's not the best time to talk, is it?'

'I can still come with you, can't I?'

She bent towards the bag on the bed, delved and pulled out her car keys. She picked the piece of paper from the pillow, slid it into her jacket pocket. 'I've got to go.'

She crossed the room, swerved round him.

He stared at the bed for a moment, rubbed a hand through his hair, then walked out onto the landing and down the stairs. Arriving in the hallway, he watched her button up her coat. She picked her powder blue beret from the hooks on the wall.

'Maybe we could talk afterwards,' he suggested.

Lydia opened the door then looked back at him. 'Are you coming or not?'

★

She swung a left off the main road before the town centre, avoiding the one-way system. On Queen's Road she braked to a stop, waited for a car to reverse into the driveway of one of the large red-brick semis.

He brushed an imaginary piece of fluff from his knee. 'I did want to say sorry,' he said. 'About not wanting to talk the other day.'

'Come on,' Lydia muttered to the driver in front. She turned up the air conditioning.

'Glenn's been pestering me about a publishing plan. I'm sure he knows about *The Jazz Cats.*'

She glanced at him, faced front again. The wiper blades squealed across the windscreen.

'But you're right, we do need to talk. You know, about

where we're going.'

'For God's sake, Tony,' she said, edging round the nose of the reversing car.

'I'm not even allowed to speak now, am I?' Tony said, as the car accelerated.

'I'm about to address the council.' She slowed to the junction, flipped on the indicator and hunched forward, waiting for a car to pass.

'Fine. I won't say another word.' He folded his arms, looked out of the side window. The road was clear of traffic.

'Good,' she said, pulling into the road. She clicked on the indicator again and steered right down a narrow side street with high walls rising on either side. After a tight bend, they emerged onto a large, near-empty car park. 'I just need to focus.'

On the left was a long four-storey block of flats, to the right were the public gardens, closed for the night now. Ahead of them, light spilled from the market square. She pulled into a parking space, ratcheted the handbrake, cut the engine.

Tony unclipped his seatbelt, pushed the car door open, climbed out. Occasional snowflakes drifted down among the easing sleet. Swinging the door shut, he stared back over the car toward the dark expanse of the public gardens. The peak of the bandstand was visible beyond the public toilets. Lydia surfaced above the car roof, interrupting his view. She pulled on her beret, set it at an angle.

In silence they walked past Pizza Express and onto the

Market Square, where once the farmers had brought livestock to sell. A low bass beat was pumping out of the pub. They crossed the flag-stoned square, heading towards the free-standing building by the road. There was a food bank and a Citizens Advice Bureau on the ground floor, their poster-stuck windows facing the brightly lit Indian restaurant. Rounding the building's corner, Tony eyed the recently vacated tea shop, the dirty window frames. There was a new nail bar beside it. Things had changed since he was last here.

They passed through the town hall's arched entrance, climbed the carpeted stairs, then proceeded through a pair of double doors.

The council chamber was smaller than Tony had expected. Four rows of blue plastic-seated chairs were laid out for the public, then, after a brief space, there was a horseshoe of tables.

Tony trailed Lydia along the aisle between the public seats. The councillors were already present, some sitting, reading; some standing, chatting. He didn't recognise any of them. There was a group of four people on the front row, to the right. One of them, a grey-haired woman, turned, saw Lydia, and stood.

Lydia surged forward. Tony followed, looking up at the vaulted ceiling, the exposed wooden beams.

'Exciting, isn't it?' the woman said. She glanced towards Tony, frowned meaningfully at Lydia, then leaned to a side. 'Hello, Tony. Nice to see you again.'

He forced a smile. 'Hello, Miriam.' She was one of Lydia's

friends; he'd met her a couple of times.

Lydia was talking to Phil, the big-eared man from yesterday. Beside Tony, a white-haired gent rose to his feet, tottered slightly, then patted his cravat.

'I think we've met before,' he said.

Tony searched his face, trying to place him.

'George,' the man explained. 'My wife and I had the bookshop on the high street.'

'Ah, of course, yes,' Tony said, none the wiser.

'You gave a reading at the shop once.'

'Right then, everybody,' a voice called over the low burble. 'Shall we make a start?'

George shuffled round, took his seat. Tony settled beside him, unzipped his coat.

'OK,' the chairman said, bending towards the microphone on the table. 'I call this meeting of the Town Council to order. Can I remind you all to switch off your mobile phones...'

Tony leaned forward. Along the row, Lydia and Phil were whispering to one another.

The chairman was still talking: '...remind everyone to declare any financial interests...'

'That's the chairman,' George whispered, resting against Tony's arm. 'Brian Nash. Phil thinks he's in bed with the developers.'

Tony gazed at the chairman, the thin moustache, the slicked-back hair.

'And that at the end's Bridget. District councillor. He

thinks she's bent as well.'

Tony frowned, unsure who the old chap was talking about. Was it the chestnut-haired woman in the gilet, or the younger woman with long boots?

'So we'll open up to any questions or presentations from the public,' the chairman said. 'Are there any presentations?'

'Only one,' the woman in long boots said, 'from Miss Lydia Dixon.'

Lydia raised her hand, stood. A faint smile flickered round the corners of Tony's mouth. An idea was forming.

★

Lydia had parked outside Wing Lee's, the Chinese takeaway on the high street. They hadn't lingered after her presentation; the council had moved into closed session. She'd made her excuses when the others had suggested going to the pub.

'So it's Kung Po chicken and fried rice?' Tony checked.

'That's it,' Lydia said, reaching into her coat pocket.

'Won't be long,' he said, and climbed from the car. The sleet was turning to snow; fat flakes swirled in the icy wind. He swung the car door shut and scuttled across the pavement.

The heat inside the takeaway was intense, the air thick with cooking smells. A small Chinese man stood behind the wooden counter, watching the news on a wall-mounted television. He was wearing a sweater with a wolf's face on the front. The man turned and smiled.

Tony placed his order, paid. As the Chinese man called something through the hatch into the kitchen, Tony walked across to the chairs by the wall. He briefly peered out of the window. In the car, Lydia's face was faintly lit as she tapped at the screen of her phone. He sat.

There was another man waiting, sitting with his back to the window, reading the *Daily Mail*. 'A New Dawn For Britain' the headline declared. The man's sweatshirt had a Watson's Carpets logo on it. Tony studied him for a moment, took in his features, the tired eyes, then he lowered his gaze and contemplated the distressed lino. The idea had struck him during the meeting. A novel about an In Bloom competition; set in a small town or village. He could explore the rivalries and social divisions among the competitors. There could even be a murder. Or not. Maybe better to keep it subtle, understated. Like *The Jazz Cats*. He would need to work on the details. But there definitely was something in it. He had that feeling.

He glanced out of the window. Lydia was talking into her phone. And he'd call the book *In Bloom*. He'd start shaping it as soon as he got home. But first he'd deal with this Lydia situation.

The hatch behind the counter snapped open. The Chinese man called, 'Beef with black bean and green peppers, and egg-fried rice. Sweet-and-sour chicken and fried rice.'

The carpets man stood and Tony wondered who the main characters should be.

★

They'd finished eating now. The smeared plates lay on Lydia's coffee table. Tony lounged on the sofa, replete. Lydia was in her rocking chair, her feet resting on the footstool. Eddie the cat purred on her knee as she absently stroked between his ears. The television was on in the corner, the ten o'clock news about to begin.

He glanced across at Lydia. Should he just come out with it? Or was it too soon after they'd eaten?

Lydia twisted towards him, dipped her chin. 'I think we should talk, about us,' she said.

He sat up. 'Yes,' he began, 'I've been thinking…'

'Please, Tony, let me finish.'

He raised his shoulders, let them drop.

'I do appreciate you being there tonight, but…' She looked past him for a moment, thoughtful, then met his eye. 'But I don't think it really changes anything. Do you?'

'OK?'

'It's just I'm not sure that it's really working any more. You and me.'

'Mmm…'

'We've tried, haven't we? But it's not right, is it?' she said, reasonably.

'I suppose not.'

'Mmm…' she said. 'So you do agree that it's not working.'

'To be honest,' he said, 'I've been wondering whether we should just, you know...' He turned down the corners of his mouth.

'I'm relieved, in a way.' She smiled, shyly. 'Because there's something I need to tell you.'

'You're not pregnant, are you?'

'Shut up, Tony.'

'Sorry.'

'I'm telling you this because I don't want to lie to you. And I wouldn't want you to hear it from someone else.'

'Hear what?' He could feel himself tensing.

She lowered her eyes. 'I think there might be somebody else.'

'What does that mean? Either there is or there isn't.'

'Well, we haven't done anything yet.'

He remained quiet, watching her.

'I just think we're more aligned.'

Tony sniggered. 'More aligned? What utter tosh.'

'Don't be churlish.'

'So how far's it gone?'

'We've only shared some sandwiches.'

'Is that code for something?'

'No,' she said, defensive now.

'So who is he?'

'You don't know him.'

'It's the guy from the committee, isn't it? The one with the ears.'

'He's called Phil.'

'I see.'

'Do you mind?'

He shrugged. 'I suppose not.'

She looked at him, smiled uncertainly. 'You're being very adult about this.'

'I mean, what else can I do? You and Phil are just, you know, more aligned.'

Her mouth tightened, she turned away, glaring at the television. A silence settled between them.

They'd missed the headlines now. There was an item about Brexit, the government's faltering trade negotiations.

'These clowns have no intention of getting a deal,' she said. 'It's ideological.'

Tony watched the images shift on the screen. Overall, he decided, breaking up with Lydia had been easier than he'd anticipated. It had been almost painless.

'It doesn't matter how they dress it up, leaving Europe makes absolutely no sense,' she said. 'It'll damage the economy and leave us isolated.'

A news item came on about a new flu-like illness. There were two cases in Italy now.

'I suppose it could be worse,' Tony said.

'Worse?' she scoffed. 'How could it possibly be worse? It's the biggest backward step since…since…the Corn Laws.'

Eddie the cat sat up and yawned.

'You're probably right,' Tony agreed. He considered her

profile for a moment, then looked along the room, towards the patio doors. 'Anyway.' He leaned forward, rubbed his thighs. 'I suppose I should go.'

She glanced at him, smiled slightly. Eddie stood, circled in her lap, then settled again.

'Don't get up,' he said, rising. He crossed to the lounge door, pulled it open. He looked back into the room, at the top of her head.

'Bye, Lydia,' he said, then moved out into the hallway. He collected his coat from the hooks, put it on and let himself out of the house.

The snow was falling heavily now, blurring the streetlights across the green. He pulled the door closed and walked out onto the pavement. Burying his chin into his collar, sinking his hands into his pockets, he set off towards the town centre. The snow was swirling, blowing into his face, plastering his anorak. It had begun to settle, on the rooftops, on the road. Tony smiled. So *In Bloom* it was. And now he could work on it without interruption. In the distance, the church clock chimed. Yes, he was going to do something spectacular.

If you have enjoyed *We Need to Talk*, do please help us spread the word – by posting a review on Amazon (you don't need to have bought the book there) or Goodreads; by posting something on social media; or in the old-fashioned way by simply telling your friends or family about it.

Book publishing is a very competitive business these days, in a saturated market, and small independent publishers such as ourselves are often crowded out by the big houses. Support from readers like you can make all the difference to a book's success.

Many thanks.

Dan Hiscocks
Publisher
Lightning Books

⚡ New Voices from Lightning

The Atomics

Paul Maunder

Midsummer, 1968. When Frank Banner and his wife Gail move to the Suffolk coast to work at a newly built nuclear power station, they are hoping to leave violence and pain behind them.

Gail wants a baby but Frank is only concerned with spending time in the gleaming reactor core of the Seton One power station. Their new neighbours are also 'Atomics' – part of the power station community. But Frank takes a dislike to the boorish, predatory Maynard. And when the other man begins to pursue a young woman who works in the power station's medical centre, Frank decides to intervene.

As the sun beats down relentlessly upon this bleak landscape, his demons return. A vicious and merciless voice tells him he has an obligation to protect the young woman and Frank knows just how to do it. Radiation will make him stronger, radiation will turn him into a hero... *The Atomics* is a gothic story of madness, revenge and Uranium-235.

A terrifically compulsive slice of post-war domestic noir: a vivid psychological thriller that unfolds into a strange and powerful study of male violence – Michael Hughes

Longlisted for the Caledonia Novel Award

Charity

Madeline Dewhurst

Edith, an elderly widow with a large house in an Islington garden square, needs a carer. Lauren, a nail technician born in the East End, needs somewhere to live. A rent-free room in lieu of pay seems the obvious solution, even though the pair have nothing in common.

Or do they? Why is Lauren so fascinated by Edith's childhood in colonial Kenya? Is Paul, the handsome lodger in the basement, the honest broker he appears? And how does Charity, a Kenyan girl brutally tortured during the Mau Mau rebellion, fit into the equation?

Capturing the spirited interplay between two women divided by class, generation and a deeper gulf from the past, and offering vivid flashbacks to 1950s East Africa, Madeline Dewhurst's captivating debut spins a web of secrets and deceit; it's not always obvious who is the spider and who is the fly.

A taut, fraught, stylish and important novel, drawing upon the facts and fictions of an oft-neglected moment in history – Eley Williams

A shocking, expertly plotted story about family and betrayal which keeps you guessing until the end. Much more than a page-turner, it shines a light on a brutal period of history – Emily Bullock

Humorous and heart-wrenching, impeccably researched and beautifully written, this haunting and original debut demands to be read – Lianne Dillsworth

Longlisted for the Bath Novel Award

The Girl from the Hermitage

Molly Gartland

It is December 1941, and eight-year-old Galina and her friend Vera are caught in the siege of Leningrad, eating wallpaper soup and dead rats. Galina's artist father Mikhail is helping to save the treasures of the Hermitage, whose cellars could provide a safe haven, as long as Mikhail can survive the perils of a commission from one of Stalin's colonels.

Three decades on, Galina is a teacher at the Leningrad Art Institute. What ought to be a celebratory weekend at her forest dacha turns sour when she makes an unwelcome discovery. The painting she starts that day will hold a grim significance for the rest of her life, as the old Soviet Union makes way for the new Russia and her world changes out of all recognition.

Warm, wise and utterly enthralling, Molly Gartland's debut novel guides us from the old communist era, with its obvious terrors and its more surprising comforts, into the bling of 21st-century St Petersburg. Galina's story is an insightful meditation on ageing and nostalgia as well as a compelling page-turner.

Compelling and enthralling...a convincingly authentic story, as well as a moving and thought-provoking one – NB Magazine

Stunning... Here is human survival in every form. An extraordinarily well-written book for a debut – Historical Novels Reviews

Elegantly written, an enthralling read – Yorkshire Times

Shortlisted for the Impress Prize; longlisted for the Bath Novel Award and the Blogger's Book Prize

Wolf Country

Tünde Farrand

London, 2050. The socio-economic crisis of recent decades is over and consumerism is thriving.

Ownership of land outside the city is the preserve of a tiny elite, and the rest of the population must spend to earn a Right to Reside. Ageing has been abolished thanks to a radical new approach, replacing retirement with blissful euthanasia at a Dignitorium.

When architect Philip goes missing, his wife Alice risks losing her home and her status, and begins to question the society in which she was raised. Her search for him uncovers some horrifying truths about the fate of her own family and the reality behind the new social order.

Wolf Country is a powerful dystopian vision in the spirit of *Black Mirror* and *Never Let Me Go*.

Gripping – The i Paper, top debut novels of 2019

Farrand absolutely nails dystopia and its unsettling predictions, with incredible writing – Buzz Magazine

Sci-fi in the tradition of Wyndham, with characters I really cared about, in a terrifyingly altered world – Jane Rogers

The Outsiders

James Corbett

Liverpool 1981. As the city burns during inner city riots, Paul meets two people who will change his life: Nadezhda, an elusive poet who has fallen out of fashion; and her daughter Sarah, with whom he shares an instant connection. As the summer reaches its climax his feelings for both are tested amidst secrets, lies and the unravelling of Nadezhda's past. It is an experience that will define the rest of his life.

The Outsiders moves from early-80s Liverpool, via Nadezhda's clandestine background in war-torn Europe, through to the present day, taking in the global and local events that shape all three characters.

In a powerful story of hidden histories, lost loves and painful truths ambitiously told against the backdrop of Liverpool's fall and rise, James Corbett's enthralling debut novel explores the complexities of human history and how individual perspectives of the past shape everyone's present.

www.lightning-books.co.uk